Rye or Die

A Laughing Loaf Bakery Mystery

Victoria Kazarian

Cover design by Mariah Sinclair

To Claire and Matt

Chapter One

SATURDAY, *October 18*

WE WERE GOING into the third week of a chilly-as-heck October.

It was another fall in River Grove, my town nestled in Northern California's Santa Cruz Mountain redwoods.

After spending the day inside my bakery, I was looking forward to getting outdoors where I could smell the change of seasons, hear the crunch of leaves under my feet, and smell the smoke from everyone's wood stove in the cold evening.

But in the midst of my favorite time of year, I was oblivious to the chaos this beautiful season would soon unleash on our little community.

Last weekend, my staff decorated the windows of The Laughing Loaf with leaves and pumpkins. Then my assistant baker Beck and her husband Sam drove over to nearby Gilroy to get freshly picked green and red apples. We filled baskets with them then set them out on the window seats for customers to share. The warm, homey smell was enticing.

For the front door, Beck had sketched a cartoon of a man sipping a Laughing Loaf spiced latte, with beautiful images of fall in River Grove filling a thought bubble above his head.

And this year, my little town was embracing the season in a new way.

After I closed up the bakery today, my boyfriend Nate and I would drive over to the town's green space, where volunteers were setting up for the start of River Grove's first Haunted Maze, a spooky and fun event intended to draw visitors into our quaint downtown.

My father had come by at lunch to pick up my dog, Biga, since my little chihuahua mix pup would fiercely try to defend us from any monsters or suspicious makeup-wearing actors getting ready to play their parts in the maze.

This Saturday had been busy. River Grovians had lined up early at The Laughing Loaf, families and dogs in tow, eager for hot lattes and fresh-from-the-oven pastries.

After closing, Beck and I got to work cleaning and prepping for the next day. It reminded me of when I'd started the bakery almost three years ago, and it had just been the two of us. We usually had more help, but Maeve Killoran, our Irish-born assistant bread maker, had driven up to Napa last night to work her weekend job at Pain Parisienne, which her boyfriend now managed.

Rose Wilkins, our staff member at-large, had left a few minutes ago to use her skills at the maze. As a former thrift shop employee and cosplayer, costumes and makeup were her superpowers. Before the maze's opening, she was helping craft the look of each of the creepy monsters and apparitions that would haunt the maze.

Mayor Corinne Webster—or as we called her, "Mayor C"—had been working on the maze project with Chamber of Commerce President Gordon Dabney since the beginning of the year. She'd asked Nate to take photos to promote the maze's opening night next week. Their plan was to draw people from local communities into the downtown area to support local business. I was happy to help, since this would benefit my bakery, too.

My boyfriend Nate was a wildlife photographer who had made a career of taking pictures of creatures (*not* the haunted kind). His usual subjects were birds, for framed art, publicity for conservation nonprofits, and at least one coffee table book from a famous British naturalist. Nate was happy to oblige the mayor and take a few shots to promote the maze for websites and local newspapers.

Beck groaned on her way to the fridge to take out the eggs. "Why is it all about scary things this time of year? Aren't the falling leaves and the cozy weather enough? I am *so* not going to the maze."

But scary was part of the goal. The Haunted Maze would not only be a twisty puzzle to navigate, it would be filled with things designed to pop out at the unsuspecting visitors making their way through it. One of the coordinators of this project was Peony Roberts, who was probably the closest person I had to an evil nemesis.

Peony was gatekeeper-receptionist at River Grove City Hall, and I wasn't surprised to see her in this new role. Even as receptionist she seemed to genuinely enjoy keeping people a little on edge.

"I *am* curious about the maze," I said, as I went to feed the sourdough starter in its big, gooey tub. I removed three large measuring cups of the starter and dumped in flour and water. I'd save the discarded starter in the fridge for use in some of my cookie and cracker recipes, where it would add a creamy, tangy flavor.

"I'll be going," I said as I used a large paddle to stir the starter tub. "As a downtown business owner, I should support it."

Beck sighed. "Enjoy yourself then. I'll be at home, working with choux pastry and watching Hallmark Christmas movies."

"Wait—they're out this early?" I gave her a skeptical look. "It's only October."

"Well, maybe I know where to find them," she raised her eyebrows and gave me a mysterious smile.

Beck and I finished up with our prep. I tried to figure out how to ask Beck casually about what had been obsessing her for the past few months. I know it had been stressful, for both her and her husband, Sam. They really wanted to be parents and had been trying to get pregnant for the past year.

This meant my brilliant baker would take a leave from her job for at least a few months, if not forever. Even though I couldn't imagine The Laughing Loaf without Beck, I really wanted them both to be parents, too.

"Any news in your life?" I asked casually, as she finished up the pumpkin tart filling at the mixer.

She looked up at me, her brown eyes intensely sorrowful for a moment. She put on a cheerful smile that looked forced, as she detached the mixing bowl.

"I'm trying not to think about it too much. I'm working on some new pastry ideas. I have that puff pastry class in San Francisco next month. I'm super excited about it. I'm also doing another cake for Reggie for an event at The Riverside. It's for his birthday!"

Her voice sounded upbeat, though I could tell how she

really felt. Beck was bad at faking things. If she was feeling something, we all knew it.

"My mom says if I think about other things, it'll happen before I know it," she offered up brightly, as she carried the bowl over to her work area.

I frowned as I bent down over the metal table to start my list of things to check tomorrow morning when I came in early. Beck often quoted her mother's advice, and I had to admit, I usually didn't agree with the old-school platitudes of her mother, Denise. Denise Reyes was a third-generation River Grovian and a homeschool mom. She and I couldn't be more different in our backgrounds and outlook on life.

I hoped Beck would get pregnant soon. If it wasn't that simple, she might have to look into fertility treatments. But I wasn't going to bring that up.

I quickly changed the subject.

"I can't wait to see what you're dreaming up for Reggie's party. Any ideas yet?"

She went to her tote bag in the corner and pulled out a sketch book. She brushed her dark hair behind her ears as she opened the book, an excited smile on her face.

"So here's what I'm thinking. It's a cake for Reggie's old chess-playing friends: Sarkis, Robert, Max, and Bill. They're coming up to River Grove next weekend to celebrate his seventy-eighth birthday. Most of them didn't even know Reggie was still alive, so they are *super* excited to see him. Reggie's got some really fun things planned. He wanted the cake to remind them of their old neighborhood back in Connecticut."

Beck had sketched a four-layer cake topped with a park, bordered by a hedge. Sitting in a line on a park bench were five boys who looked like they were eleven or twelve. I wondered if Reggie had given Beck a photo to work from.

The faces Beck had sketched were full of personality: smirks, smiles, and scowls. Normal expressions a group of middle school boys would have.

The one on the end, a kid with painfully short black hair and black-rimmed glasses, had to be The Riverside's owner, Reggie McFerrin—or as he was known back then, Leonard Reginald Fortiner. There was an amused look on his face that I recognized immediately.

Reggie would enjoy himself, as he renewed old ties. At least, I *hoped* this would be a pleasant event for him.

Last night after closing, I sat down with Reggie, owner of The Riverside Saloon, over coffee. I was one of the few people he'd confided in as he reconnected with the life he'd left behind sixty years ago, in his rebellion against an over-bearing father.

"You're going to start sharing your new—uh, *old*—identity."

"With just a trusted few," he said with an amused nod. "I'm not in a rush."

Which was good—and also very Reggie.

Having his oldest, closest friends in town to celebrate was a good first step. They'd talk about old times, share about their lives over the past sixty years. And play chess, of course, since one of the big revelations about Reggie's past was that he'd been a highly ranked chess champion. My chess-playing dad had received an invitation to the party just for that purpose. Terrified of Reggie's competitive friends, he'd been practicing moves and strategies for the past month.

"Reggie will love this," I told Beck as she closed her sketch book. "Please, take a picture of the cake when you're finished."

Beck smiled softly as she put the book away. "I will,

Gracie. And thanks for encouraging me to do this. I'm not 100 percent sure I know what I'm doing, but if people are willing to put up with what I make—I'm happy to make it. I'm getting better at not second-guessing myself."

If people are willing to put up with what I make?

I internally rolled my eyes at that. As long as I'd known her, Beck had shown an effortless skill and creativity in every kind of baking she took on.

We'd worked together well since the beginning of The Laughing Loaf, even though the two of us were wired very differently: Beck was an artist, with her creativity and grasp of flavors. I was more of a tactician, a puzzle solver. I ran the bakery, crunched the data to keep it profitable, and solved the occasional crime that happened in our little town.

After a few moments of low confidence, Beck was taking on everything she baked with excitement and, for the most part, fearlessness.

"Look at you, Beck," I said with admiration. "There's something different about your cakes. They're whimsical and they make people smile. But they also make them think." I looked her in the eye, smiling just a little. "You know most cakes don't make people *think*, right?"

"All I know is, doing this makes me happy," Beck said cheerfully as she continued filling tart shells.

Once Beck had finished up her tarts and cleaned her work area, she put on her jacket and shouldered her tote bag.

"I'll work on this a little more tonight. See you tomorrow bright and early, Gracie!"

Not long after Beck left, I was surprised to see Rose come through the back door, breathless. She reached for her long wool coat and scarf on the coat rack. "It's really cold in the green space. I'm shivering so hard I can't apply makeup."

"Thanks for the warning. Nate and I will bundle up." I looked at the clock on the wall. "We'll see you soon."

"Gracie, do you need me any earlier tomorrow? It'll be Sunday, and I thought you might, since Maeve won't be here to help with the bread, and you've got those rye and harvest loaves in the mix now."

"That would be helpful. How about 6:00 a.m.? Beck would also love the help, since you've gotten the beignet process down."

At the word beignet, Rose broke into a smile. "That part will be my reward. I can't get enough of those things."

With a bounce in her step, Rose wrapped her neck with a thick scarf, hand-embroidered with daisies and pink skulls, and headed out the back door into the cold dusk.

I sat back on the stool at the metal table and let out a sigh of relief, looking around at my very tidy baking room. I took in the tantalizing smell of pumpkin tarts redolent with rich, warm spices, then our usual layered scones, smelling rich and buttery, and loaves of earthy whole grain bread rising in the proofer.

The bakery had gone through big changes this year. We'd finished a major remodel this summer and started a lunch service. I'd hired five new staff members. Not only were they good at their jobs, their friendliness and sense of humor made the bakery a better place.

I took in my breath as I walked to the front counter to clear out the display case. I thought of the lively gathering place my bakery had become since I'd opened it, not long after we relocated to River Grove.

Everything was going so well, I wanted to hold on to everything just as it was now. I knew that wasn't realistic.

People change, and their lives follow different paths according to their dreams. They connect for a while, veer away, and, if you're lucky, they reconnect—like Reggie was doing with his old friends. My own story was a little different. I was in River Grove because I'd relocated here under federal witness protection. I might never reconnect with my past.

But I was fine with that.

How could I explain the incredible upgrade my life had undergone since moving to this town?

Gone were my days of enforcing deadlines as a software project manager in Seattle, and I was no longer married to an egotistical man who sold defense secrets on the sly. I lived in a quaint, friendly town.

And my ex, Ben Morrison, was now housed in a maxi mum-security prison in Florence, Colorado.

Instead of pressuring programmers to meet their deadlines, I now baked things that made people happy.

I shut down my computer and turned off the lights in the dining area, leaving the hanging Edison lights on over the front counter.

I heard a knock at the front door, and in the fading light, saw my boyfriend Nate's grinning face at The Laughing Loaf's front door.

I took off my apron, grabbed my purse, and ran to let him in the front door.

He came in, shut the door behind him, and gave me a good long kiss on the lips in the dim light of the dining area.

Two teenage boys carrying backpacks walked past the window, slowed down, and finally stopped in their tracks to watch us.

"I'll show them how it's done," Nate said, with a

mischievous grin. He put his arm around me, leaned me back gracefully, and went for another kiss.

The boys gawked at us, jaws dropped, then looked at each other and started smirking. They paused for a moment to see if we'd do anything else. Disappointed, they moved on.

"Are you sure you're a good influence on the youth of River Grove?" I said as I recovered my upright stance.

"From what I've seen walking through the green space after school lets out, these kids need to work on their finesse." Nate chuckled. "Maybe my techniques can help them. It's my public service."

Nate's Volvo was parked outside on the street. After I locked the front door, he opened the door of his Volvo for me. I slid into the nice warm car.

As I sat there, I was surprised to see a nicely dressed couple unlock the door at the old Loudon's Antique Emporium next door. I was startled to see anything going on there, since the business had closed two years ago after the arrest of its owner. There had been a FOR SALE sign up for months.

"Looks like something's happening next door," I said. "Maybe the place finally sold."

Nate buckled his seatbelt. "Brad Castro just told me a developer bought it. They're splitting it into units to lease."

"Maybe we'll get some good neighbors," I said, watching vague movement behind Loudon's dirty display window.

I wondered how long it would take to clear the grime, dust, and second-rate antiques out of the building. Two years ago, I'd had a scary confrontation there with jewel thieves that still gave me chills.

"I don't know what to expect from this maze," Nate said

as he started the car. "I'm going for some good action shots, something that grabs people's attention."

We drove toward The Riverside in fading daylight, on an evening when it looked like the town had shut down early so everyone could flee to their nice, warm houses.

It was a short four blocks down to The Riverside's green space.

Nate looked over at me. "Are you going to be warm enough, Gracie?"

I was wearing a flannel-lined jean jacket, but I was shivering even with the car heater on.

"I've got my big down jacket in the back," he said, as he drove down the street in the direction of The Riverside. "You'll be lost in it, but it'll keep you warm."

As soon as he parallel parked on the street in front of The Riverside's spacious, redwood-lined park area, Nate got out of the car and went to his trunk. He brought out a large navy blue down jacket and handed it to me when I stepped out of the car.

I slid my arms into the jacket, which drooped down over my thighs. I rolled up the sleeves so I could see my hands. I instantly felt warmer. Nate's jacket, like all of his outdoor wear, was rated for below-zero temperatures in the Sierras.

"Better?" He nodded to me, trying not to laugh.

"I feel like the Michelin Man," I chuckled. "But I'm nice and warm."

We looked across the evolving landscape in front of us.

Over the past two weeks, The Riverside's spacious green space had been transforming. Black partitions had been set up, looking like someone was building a house out of very large dominos. Every day it got bigger and longer.

Tonight, floodlights beamed over the space, covering the team of workers in bright silver light, like a road crew at work on a highway after hours. I recognized a few of my teenage Laughing Loaf regulars: Dakota Li, Amelia Gruber, and class clown Sky Robbins' little brother, Jack. They were draping what looked like moss over the walls of the maze.

Over to the side, at a folding table, Rose sat across from a young man whose longish hair was pulled back into a ponytail. She leaned over as she shaded his green face with a darker green to give him a hollowed out, zombified look.

"Hi, Gracie!" Rose called out with the wave of a makeup brush as she saw me.

Nate, who already had his camera out, circled the brightly lit area and began taking shots of the young man. Nate had a look I recognized: focused and in the zone as he framed his shots.

I pulled up a chair and sat down at the table across from Rose.

"Looking good, Rose," I said as she leaned over the young man, brushing black on his brows to create a unibrow.

"Just wait. I haven't even done the gross part yet," she said, focusing intently as she dabbed her brush across the middle of the young man's brows. "I'm going to create a *trompe l'oeil* effect on his forehead to make it look like part of his skin is peeled back. I've done it once before. It should look pretty cool."

"Will this be hard for me to wipe off?" The tentative, high-pitched voice of the teen zombie piped up. His voice was such a contrast to the scary makeup, I let out a giggle.

"Use some of your sister's makeup remover on it, Lucas. When you've got most of it off, scrub your face with soap and a washcloth. You'll be fine for school on Monday."

The young man looked worried.

"But I'm hanging out with friends tomorrow. They're going to think it looks stupid."

Rose snorted, amused. "Threaten to eat their brains. I wouldn't worry about it."

Nate had taken a few close-ups of our zombie, then had moved over to the maze to snap some photos. Mayor C had just arrived, carrying a creepy clown about the same height as her. When she set it down in front of the maze entrance, Nate moved over to focus on the leering prop.

"I wonder if the mayor's thought about including a haunted version of Runty the Rat." I watched the mayor cower in mock fear as Nate bent down to get some shots. Runty was the beloved mascot of the River Rats, our town's softball team.

Rose laughed, her eyes still focused on the young man's face.

"You've got to suggest that, Gracie. Mayor C takes her softball team so seriously. I think it would be hilarious."

Then I heard a voice that didn't exactly strike fear in me, more like annoyance.

"*Nice*, Gracie," Peony Roberts drawled, giving me a slow clap from where she stood near the maze.

Tonight, Peony's hair was done up in two giant braid loops, topped by a black wool beret pulled down to her eyebrows. With the black-and-white striped shirt she was wearing, she looked like a French mime. "You've actually come up with a good idea while managing to distract our makeup artist from her job," Peony continued. "I'll talk to Corinne about including Runty. We've got the costume. Might as well use it. Everyone knows Runty. Who wouldn't love *Zombie* Runty?"

With that, Peony headed over toward Mayor C. Nate

was directing the mayor as she posed for shots at the maze entrance.

I followed Peony, my arms folded over my chest. Nate's down jacket felt like a tent on me, but it was doing its job.

"So what exactly do you do with the maze, Peony? What are your responsibilities?"

Peony gave me a solemn look, her chin tilted high. "The mayor has put me in charge of staffing and security. I'm the human resources department."

I almost rolled my eyes. Human resources seemed about as safe a task for Peony as spraying a fire with a fine mist of gasoline. Tact was not her strong point.

"How many people are working on this project?"

"We've got forty-three. Builders and decorators, then the actors and guides—who'll be there for our performances. By Tuesday night, we should be completely done with construction and decoration. Wednesday's our dress rehearsal—then Friday we're open for business."

"This is quite a production Peony," I said. "I'm looking forward to seeing this when it all comes together."

"We're counting on everyone getting the word out." Peony listened for a moment as Mayor C pointed out other areas of the maze for Nate to photograph. "That means you, Gracie. You're a downtown merchant and you have a big role to play. Talk this up to your customers. Especially customers from out of town."

"I have been. The teenagers are already on board."

In the corner of my eye, I saw Nate squat down and focus his camera up at a scaly dragon tail draped across the top of a maze corridor.

Peony left to go talk to a group working on a side display for younger maze visitors—a few toddler-sized witches and fairies were playing hide-and-go-seek behind a patch of large foam pumpkins and toadstools.

I glanced back at Rose and her zombie. She'd started in on the skull part on the young man's head and was outlining a peeled-back flap of skin. It was realistic enough to make my skin crawl. Peony had chosen the maze's makeup artist wisely.

I watched Mayor C leaning in toward Nate, gesturing, as he took his shots. I walked over to them, thinking a little distraction might nip the mayor's micromanagement in the bud.

I genuinely liked and admired Mayor C. She was tough, obsessed with protecting River Grovians, and tried to make our town a better place in any way she could—even if it sometimes gave us all a lot more work to do.

Mayor C gestured down the corridor as she explained to Nate. "What we need is a shot looking down into the maze entrance, so you see the long spider legs hanging over the edge of the maze. Once we get the motor set up, the legs will move."

"I can do that, Corinne," Nate said, doing a nice job of redirecting the mayor on his own. "What might also work is if you have somebody in the maze, cowering under the spider legs in a shot looking down from above. Peony might be a good person to do that."

The mayor considered this, then called Peony over.

"Do exactly what Nate tells you to do," the mayor told Peony gruffly as she approached.

Nate explained the shot to the young woman, and she went around to the opening of the maze.

Even at six foot, four inches, Nate had to pull over a crate to stand on, to look over the high partition. I soon saw his head pop up over the wall. He aimed his lens down at the terrified-looking Peony.

Peony's muffled voice drifted up from inside the maze. "How about if I crouch down and look like I'm screaming?"

"Perfect," Nate said, as he angled his camera over the maze wall. He took a series of shots.

"Awesome, Peony," he called. "Now back up against that opposite wall and look up like you've just been surprised by the spider."

Peony must have nailed it, because Nate started laughing as his camera reeled off shots. "You got it, Peony. Thanks."

Peony came out of the end of the maze, flipped a braid loop over her shoulder cooly and went back to address a group of teen volunteers, as if she did this kind of thing every day.

Nate came over to me, laughing to himself.

"Peony played along nicely, and it's a good setup. I got some winners."

Nate found Mayor C and told her he'd get shots to her by tomorrow morning. When he came back, I realized I was really hungry. As usual, in the rush of the day, I hadn't gotten lunch.

My father was at home, boning up on his chess strategies, since he'd face tough competition at Reggie's birthday party on Friday. I'd warned him not to forget to cuddle with Biga—and let him out in back to run around and do his thing.

"Up for dinner at The Riverside?" I shoved my hands into the jacket pockets to keep warm. "I'm starving—and freezing."

"I don't know, hon. It's such a long walk." Nate looked over at The Riverside's front door, just twenty feet away from us. He laughed as he twisted the large lens off his camera and put his equipment away in his camera bag.

As the workplace of Mayor C and River Grove Police Chief Dave Westerman, City Hall might be where decisions were made in River Grove, but The Riverside was the heart of our town.

As a restaurant, music venue, and inn, The Riverside was where people came to gather, go on dates, get good food and drinks, and dance. Kirk Schiffer, my best friend's husband and CEO of the software company BlueSoft, even worked out business deals here over drinks.

I reached for Nate's warm hand, and we walked across the green space together toward the music venue. Music thumped as we approached, probably the opening band for whoever was headlining tonight. Everything I loved was in this moment—music, the smell of delicious food, and Nate's warm hand in mine. I breathed in the crisp air.

We opened the double doors and walked into The Riverside's main hall.

When a hostess came up to seat us, Nate nodded.

"We don't need a dining table," he told her. "We're here for drinks and some appetizers."

She waved us on to the bar area. Drake, our usual bartender, wasn't there tonight and had been replaced by a man I'd seen working a few times—a short, middle-aged fellow with greying hair, Carson.

"Gracie, Nate. It's good to see you. There's a high table at the end there, if you'd like to sit. What can I get you?"

"I'd like an Irish Coffee with whipped cream." I shivered. "I need to warm up."

Nate thought about it. "Give me your best IPA on tap."

I ordered us chips, guacamole (Reggie's own recipe), and a plate of chicken and veggie combo sliders.

"Who's playing tonight?" Nate asked Carson.

"A rock trio from LA, called Kipper Taylor and the Bad Blood," Carson said as he squirted Nate's IPA into a mug. "Reggie says they've got a big cult following down south. The opener right now is some local kids from over in Ben Lomond—honestly can't remember their name but they're good."

Carson handed us our drinks, and we made our way to the table, which gave us a perfect view of the band—not close enough to be blasted by the music, but near enough to enjoy it and even to dance, if my dancing boyfriend felt moved to get up and do his thing.

We sat down, and with my feet dangling from the high table, I felt like a little kid as I swung my legs. Not being on my feet felt wonderful.

"The mayor says online ticket sales for the maze have exceeded her expectations," I said. "They built up a buzz and they're getting orders from the valley and the coast. The Chamber of Commerce is calling it a success."

Nate took a sip of his IPA and got a fluffy line of foam on his mustache. It was so cute in combination with the serious look on his face, I didn't want to tell him.

"My shots tonight will go on the website and to the news outlets. They're promoting the hell out of this maze."

"Seems like it's working. I think the mayor's found a new partner to scheme with."

Nate frowned and then let out a laugh. "Don't tell me that Corinne and the chief have broken up? Is public safety not her true love anymore?" From the first days of my bakery, Mayor C and the chief had come in every morning to sit down and work on lowering the crime rate and making sure our town's streets were safe. But last year the two had a falling out over an arrest he made.

I waved my hand. "Those two are just fine. They'll always have their disagreements. It's just that Corinne's new mission in life is to help downtown businesses. Part of that is because Maeve's been living at Mayor C's during the week. Maeve tells her what's going on with the bakery, and that's helped the mayor understand what it's like to run a business in River Grove."

Nate nodded. "Funny how things work out like that. Well, I'm glad. I hope the haunted maze puts River Grove on the map."

Our appetizers arrived and we dug in. With a bowl of Reggie's guacamole, I was in my happy place. He'd developed the recipe over his years in River Grove. It was creamy, garlicky, tangy, with just the right amount of spice.

Nate practically inhaled his slider then reached for another, looking like a giant devouring a tiny peasant's dinner. He tapped the table in time to the music. "I've got that shoot in Oregon next week on the Deschutes River. I'll be gone for a week. Want to do something special when I get back?"

"We're busy with Halloween coming up, but I can plan for that and talk to Beck. Rose is off early to work at the maze, so we're a little thin on coverage."

Nate nodded. "Let's do something simple then, after Halloween. I love going away on these shoots, but—" he turned pink "I do find I miss you more now. It's harder for me to be away that long."

Work travel was a fact of life for Nate, and I admitted it was hard for me to see him gone that long, too. On the other hand, I focused more on my bakery when he was away. I threw myself into my work. It wasn't like I didn't miss him. But I got more organization and planning done when he was gone.

We finished our sliders as we listened to the boys from Ben Lomond. They had a lot of energy, that's for sure. The wiry, freckled frontman-guitarist leaped around Mick Jagger–style as he played in front of the quiet, sedate diners. The shaggy-haired drummer looked like he was about 15. I don't think I'd ever seen anyone hit a drum kit that hard.

As we sat tapping our feet, I saw something out of the corner of my eye a few tables away from us. Two men were having dinner while discussing something related to the papers they'd laid out on the table. The younger was dressed in expensive casual wear, his dark hair in what looked like a very expensive haircut. The older man, probably in his fifties, wore jeans and a sports team hoodie and looked like he'd just stepped away from his kid's soccer practice.

If The Riverside was a place where deals were struck over food and drinks, could these guys be planning the newest Silicon Valley startup? Or launching a new local business?

"What do you think those two are up to?" I asked, leaning my chin on my hand as I tried to keep my eyes open. I'd been up since 4:30 a.m., and I was starting to fade.

"They don't look like locals. Maybe they're launching a new company. Or one of them is trying to sell the other some service." Nate leaned back in his chair, trying to watch surreptitiously. We both liked to observe people and tell stories about who they were and what they were doing.

I watched as the older one of the men frowned, then raised his voice.

"Don't think I haven't seen what you've been doing behind my back," he barked. "We were friends. I've put everything into helping you with this venture, now you've gone ahead and—."

Suddenly the Ben Lomond drummer launched into a thunderous drum fill, banging on the low tom drums with all he had, and blocking out the rest of what the man said.

"Damn, that kid's loud," Nate groaned. "I completely missed that."

"Just when it was getting interesting," I sighed as I turned to my phone to check text messages. The language between the two men, whom I observed had a definite tech bro vibe, made me glad I was running a bakery now and not working for a software company.

"Hold on. The older guy's getting up," Nate said, as the man in a hoodie put on his baseball cap, an angry look on his face.

"Why are you blaming me? Your problems are your own damn fault," the still-seated man yelled back.

The words hung in the air as the older man stomped toward The Riverside's double doors, and made his way out into the cold night air.

The younger man sat at the table and laughed to himself as he watched his table partner leave. Then he calmly walked up to the bar and settled the bill.

I turned to Nate as we stood up to go pay our bill at the bar.

"As Kirk Schiffer says, tech partnerships can be made over a dinner and just as easily broken."

He frowned. "It sounds like there's more going on here than just a business deal."

We chatted with Reggie McFerrin, who'd come downstairs just as we headed toward the door. His brown eyes looked warm and friendly. I could actually *see* them now. He hadn't worn his classic aviator sunglasses since the chess tournament in August when his old life had been revealed.

Sunglasses had been his standard wear since I'd known

him. I did a double take every time I saw him now. I still wasn't used to seeing his eyes, though I had to say he looked happier.

"People working on the maze have been coming in for dinner or drinks afterwards," Reggie said with a chuckle. "I feel a little selfish. We may be the business helped most by the haunted maze. And it hasn't even opened yet."

"That's not a bad thing," Nate said, giving Reggie a man hug. "By the way, is it 'happy birthday' yet?"

"Not till Friday. My friends get into town Thursday night. I may have a few of you friends over at another time, so stay tuned for more details."

As soon as we walked out into the night, my breath started freezing. I watched it drift up in the glow of The Riverside's front lights. I felt for Nate's hand next to me and tucked mine into his. As much as it made me shiver, I loved the cold and would much rather wrap up and endure it than deal with the heat of summer.

He squeezed my hand as we walked slowly back past the maze, still highlighted by floodlights. It had been embellished with a few more structural details in the past hour. Cobwebs and fake moss trailed down the sides of the maze walls. Mayor C's evil-eyed clown stood in front of the opening of the maze like a sentry, his red mouth turned up in a taunting grin.

The actors and set builders had left. Rose was by herself, earbuds in, listening to music on her phone as she packed up makeup boxes and mirrors at the folding table nearby.

"Need help carrying your things?" I asked her after she'd taken out her buds. She looked energized after her makeup session, even though she'd come into work at dawn this morning.

"Yeah, thanks." She smiled. "Mayor C had to take off early tonight. She left about twenty minutes ago."

"You were out here alone? It's pretty late," Nate said with a frown.

"I'm used to being out late, so it doesn't bother me," Rose said with a smile. "The last actor I worked on left just ten minutes ago. I've been fine." She directed a sheepish look at me. "Uh, I realize I *do* have to get up early, however."

Nate grabbed the large makeup kit and one of the big mirrors, and I picked up a tote bag.

In the stillness, I heard a strange noise. A low moan and scratching, like an animal rooting around.

"What's that noise?" I looked at Nate. "Do you guys hear that?"

"I heard it. Maybe a coyote trying to get at a small animal." He closed his eyes to listen.

Rose shivered. "I've had my ear buds in. But now that I hear it, it does sound like it's coming from the maze."

Fear rippled through me. It was dark, late, and my brain was tired. I didn't feel like going into a space designed to disorient and confuse people.

Now we heard something louder: a low, guttural moaning. Nate, Rose, and I looked at each other.

"That does not sound like an animal," I said with a catch in my voice.

Nate nodded and pressed his lips together in a firm line. He pulled out his phone and turned on its light.

"Let's check this out," he said.

We set down Rose's boxes and mirror on the table.

The first thing we saw was the creepy clown at the maze entrance, beckoning us to enter his twisted lair.

Foolishly, we walked right past him into the darkness of the maze.

Chapter Two

SATURDAY NIGHT, *October 18*

WITHOUT THE FLOODLIGHTS, the maze was completely black, except for the tiny spotlight cast by Nate's phone.

I tried to calm my breathing so I could hear any noise or groan from inside the maze. Any movement, however subtle.

We continued into the maze's main opening. Thick spider webs draped across the top of the corridor above us, blocking out any outside light. Claw marks slashed across the walls, signs of a werewolf perhaps.

Suddenly, we came face to face with a dead end. One of many we'd find as we tried to navigate the maze.

"I'm hearing it again, louder," Nate whispered next to me. His ears were attuned to the sounds of nature more than mine, since he was always on the trail of birds or other small creatures to photograph.

Then I heard it: a scraping, clawing noise on wood around a corner just ahead, or so I thought. I tried to figure out how to get to that noise, but when we got nearer to where I thought the noise was coming from, we faced another black plywood panel in front of us. Another dead end. There seemed no way to get directly to the noise.

Rose moved to the front. "I think if we can find a way to go left, it turns back in that direction of the sound. At least that's what I'm remembering."

I had a dim memory of being in a hedge maze as a kid years ago on a visit to England with my parents.

If you consistently keep one hand on the surface next to you and follow it, you will find your way out.

This was all I had to go on.

I placed my right hand on the right wall and kept it there as we moved forward. The wall turned to the right, then quickly made a switch to the left, but I kept my same hand on the wall, following it.

We moved forward and sure enough, there was a passageway to our left. We hurried down it, and in about ten feet, we were faced with two choices: turning to the right or continuing straight ahead. We decided to go straight ahead.

Disorientation came over me like a thick fog on the highway to the coast. I had no idea where we were now.

"I don't hear it now," I said weakly, my legs and feet starting to ache after a long day.

"Me, either," Rose breathed, stopping to listen.

I wondered if we were following nothing but our own late-night hallucinations, driven by weariness. In some way, we were maze testers tonight.

I felt lost, tired, cold, and disoriented. So, hey, the maze had done what it was designed to do. I'd stopped following the wall with my hand. We weren't trying to get to the maze's exit; we were trying to find the source of a sound inside the maze.

I pulled my scarf up around my neck as I felt the damp chill penetrate Nate's jacket.

Nate stopped and stood for a moment. He closed his eyes, as if trying to picture our progress into the maze to this point. Rose covered a yawn with her hand.

We faced another blank wall, now at a juncture where our choices were right or left.

Nate looked to the left.

"This way." He took a deep breath.

We cautiously crept forward, following the light from Nate's phone like a clump of nearsighted moths.

"I heard some movement," Nate said, speeding up. "And another groan."

Before the next left turn, we stopped before proceeding into a short corridor that ended suddenly.

That's when we saw it.

The crumpled body of the younger man sitting a few tables away from us at The Riverside. It looked like he'd been shot in the chest.

While Nate tried to resuscitate the man, I called 911. At least our phone service worked, though I had no idea how to tell the dispatcher to find us inside the maze.

Rose and I rigged up a flag using her scarf and Nate's tripod. This flag and its mast stood about a foot above our position in the maze. I heard a siren, then the sound of a truck pulling up.

"This isn't working," Nate said as he sat back on his heels. "He has no pulse. And he's lost a lot of blood." He stood up and tried to look out over the maze walls. The designer had done a brilliant job. It was hard for my tall boyfriend to see over the tops of the walls. He wouldn't be able to trace a path out—or describe a route in for anyone to follow to our location.

In a few minutes, I heard a buzzing noise, which, to my tired brain, sounded like a large insect descending on us from above.

"It's a drone," Nate said as he looked up.

Soon, we heard heavy footsteps coming toward us, and within a minute, saw the face of Deputy Brad Castro, drone controller in his hands, followed by EMTs with a medical kit and a stretcher.

After the EMTs lifted the body onto the stretcher, Brad led everyone out of the maze, guided by his drone and phone camera.

There was nothing we could do for the man we found in the maze. While he must have still been alive when we entered the maze to find him, he'd lost too much blood. The EMTs told us he must have been lying in the maze for about twenty minutes.

The chief joined us at Rose's table near the maze entrance. He rubbed his eyes and looked down at his phone. He held up a plastic bag containing the man's wallet.

"Name's Jeremy Bradshaw. CEO of Generistic—a new tech company across the hill in Sunnyvale. Only 42. Judging by his photo collection, he has a wife and young kids."

I thought about the conversation Nate and I had overheard. About the business deal the older man had been talking to him about—and then the older man's outrage at something he'd found out Jeremy had done.

"Chief, Nate and I saw him and an older man arguing in The Riverside. The older man was trying to help Jeremy with something related to a business deal. Apparently, the older man discovered Jeremy had been doing something behind his back."

The chief raised his eyebrows.

"Any name for the other man—this older man arguing with him?"

I shook my head. "Nate and I just happened to be people-watching. It was hard not to listen in on their conversation. But no, we didn't hear any name for the older man."

Separately, Nate and I gave our descriptions of him. The chief typed info into his tablet.

"Maybe Reggie can get me a name from a credit card transaction. I'll check with him."

Another murder in our little town. The only thing that consoled me in any way was that this man wasn't from River Grove. Still, it happened here, and I hated that we were developing a reputation as Murder Capital, USA—or, at least, Murder Capital of the Santa Cruz Mountains.

Deputy Brad joined us, carrying his drone. He and the chief took each of us aside separately and asked us questions.

Nate, being Nate the Boy Scout, looked upset after being questioned by the chief.

"If we'd gotten to him sooner, we might have been able to do more for him." He shook his head. "He might have had a chance."

The chief put a hand to Nate's arm. "You couldn't have, son. The EMTs said he'd lost too much blood, and with the chest wound it would be fast. The delay in getting to him wouldn't have made a difference."

Nate frowned and looked down.

My brain had already begun teasing this bizarre crime,

pulling it apart. Why would the killer have chosen to shoot him in the maze?

"Maybe the killer *knew* it would take longer to find the man if he shot him here. Maybe they were counting on that. It gave him time to get away from the area—as long as *he* could get out okay."

The chief shrugged as he looked down at the body. "You could be right, Gracie."

Nate drove Rose and I back to The Laughing Loaf, in the still, dark night. The air was rich with fall scents, and the stars glittering in the clear black sky were as beautiful as they always were, but it all had a dark, ominous feel now.

We made sure Rose got her makeup boxes and tools back to her car in The Riverside parking lot.

Nate kissed me on the forehead before he got into his car. He looked shaken. And distant.

"I need to go home and clean up after this," he said with a deep sigh as he looked down at his bloody hands. "I'd like to meet tomorrow night for dinner before I head up to Oregon on Monday. Let's do my house this time."

The thought of a quiet dinner, without my father or his girlfriend Mary Jo, sounded wonderful.

Nate locked the doors and started the car. We headed for my house, on a drive that was silent.

After being awake for sixteen hours, I should have had thoughts of sleep, but my mind was still lost somewhere in the dark, twisting maze.

I wondered if Nate and I had witnessed the setup to Jeremy Bradshaw's murder.

Chapter Three

Saturday night, *October 18*

Back home, my father sat in his recliner, watching a YouTube video on opening chess moves in preparation for Reggie's birthday party.

Biga lay curled up in his lap. When my little dog heard me come in, he poked his head up.

"How is the maze coming along, dear?"

I plopped down on the sofa across from him, let out a tired groan, and told him about our experience finding the body in the maze.

Maybe it was the fact that he was used to hearing me come home to announce a murder, but my father seemed much more interested in the maze than in the body we'd found.

"Fascinating," he said, as he tapped his pointer finger on his chin. "Somebody killed a man in a maze—or at least left a body in one. If they'd gotten lost, they'd be in a lot of trouble; they had to be sure of their ability to get out after committing the murder."

I nodded. "I wondered if that was the case."

"There are some simple techniques to figuring out a maze," my dad said.

"Like what?" I asked, as Biga jumped down from the recliner and followed me to the sofa. He hopped up and made himself quite comfortable as he settled in my lap.

"Did you try keeping your hand on the wall and following it?" he asked.

"I did, but after a while I decided it didn't make sense. We weren't trying to get out." With my dad's experience with puzzles and brain teasers, I'd been expecting a more complicated and mathematical solution.

"How about Ariadne's Thread, from mythology?" My father sat up excitedly. "She gave Theseus a ball of thread to use, to unravel as he went through the Minotaur's labyrinth. The idea is to mark your route through the maze, so you know where you've been and what's been successful." My dad sat, lost in thought, as he contemplated this. "Interesting that this is also a technique that AI uses in chess games. It retraces moves so you can go back to where you started and try alternative moves."

"I'm not sure we were in a very logical state of mind as we tried to follow the sounds we heard." I rubbed Biga's head, and he climbed up onto my stomach to get more of it. "The thing is, Nate and I saw the man not long before that. He sat a few tables away from us at The Riverside. He was arguing with an older man, who'd helped him with something business related. The older man claimed the younger guy did something serious, but we couldn't hear what it was."

My dad's eyes lit up. "Maybe the answer to this murder fell into your lap tonight. The older man did it."

Could it be that clear cut? It was possible the case would be solved easily within a day or so, without any help from me. Maybe the perpetrator would be caught and confess he'd done it in a fit of anger. Which would bode well for me getting back to business at The Laughing Loaf. I'd been helping the chief investigate murders in River Grove for the past two years, but it often took time away from my duties at my busy bakery.

The chief and Deputy Castro would follow up with Reggie at The Riverside to see what information they could get on the identity of the older man at the table.

"It could be that there's a lot more to the story than what we heard," I said, musing as I cuddled Biga. "Oh, tomorrow night, I'll be going to Nate's for dinner, since he's taking off the next morning for his shoot in Oregon."

"I've got a tutoring session with a couple of River Grove High students—and a date afterwards," my father said. "Mary Jo and I are going to have a potluck here when I get back."

What a cozy picture, the two of them sitting down to partake of their tiny buffet, asking each other the significance of their dish. "You know, that's a *very* small potluck, dad."

"I'm making salade Niçoise," he said, as he shut down his laptop. "Like your mother used to make. Mary Jo's making chicken cordon bleu."

"That's some pretty fancy cooking," I said, remembering how delicious that salad had been. My father's culinary prowess was growing. I'd only started teaching him how to cook for himself a year ago—mostly so *I* didn't have to cook everything. It had helped a lot.

As their relationship progressed, Mary Jo had taken over my dad's culinary education. The two of them made dinners together and he was constantly challenged to improve his culinary game. He'd come a long way from the guy who'd acted helpless while struggling to make toast. After a quick check of my phone messages, I went back to my room, followed by Biga. The body at the maze had shaken me, and I wondered how much sleep I'd get tonight.

My phone vibrated with a text from my closest friend in River Grove, Elana Schiffer. Of course she'd be contacting me. Elana had a very deep need to be in the loop.

Kirk heard there's been a murder at The Riverside. WHAT IS UP?

Give me the lowdown, girl

I CALLED her and told her what Nate and I had seen at The Riverside at dinner and then in the maze.

"Well, that seems too obvious," Elana said. "The older man is the killer."

"Maybe." I rubbed my eyes, thinking I should probably get to bed soon.

"Wait a minute. I don't remember you saying the victim's name." Elana said suddenly.

"Oh, yeah. He was Jeremy Bradshaw. A software guy, a CEO for some startup in Silicon Valley."

There was a long pause on the line, something that didn't happen often with my talkative friend.

"Gracie," she said in a sober voice. "Kirk and I went to

dinner with him and his wife just last week. We've been friends with Jeremy and Amy for years."

Chapter Four

SATURDAY NIGHT, *October 18*

IF I SUSPECTED I wasn't going to get a good night's sleep before I talked to Elana, I really wasn't going to get one now.

Lying next to my leg, Biga looked up at me, annoyed, as I peppered Elana with questions.

Seriously? How long are you going to talk this time?

After Elana gave me the details of their dinner with the Bradshaws, I told her I needed to get some sleep and we said goodnight.

So what did I really do? I pulled my laptop over from my nightstand and opened it.

I typed Jeremy Bradshaw into the Google search box.

Immediately a flurry of articles and photos popped up onto my screen.

First, there were popular search topics for the guy:

Jeremy Bradshaw AI startup
Jeremy Bradshaw married?
Jeremy Bradshaw net worth
Jeremy Bradshaw age
Jeremy Bradshaw workout routine

All these topics meant this guy was someone a lot of women (and probably men) had been curious about.

I looked closely at the photos and thought back to the man we'd seen at The Riverside.

The man in the photos was buff, had thick, expensively cut dark hair, and wore clear framed glasses. He had a Clark Kent look—like all he had to do was whip off his glasses and he could take to the sky and rescue a city.

The more I read about his company, the more intrigued I was. I wasn't an expert on AI, but I was skeptical about the claims the company was making about itself.

NEW CONTENDER ENTERS AI STAGE
GENERISTIC to usher in "safe and honest" era of AI, Bradshaw claims

At this point in time, AI was a source of fear and distrust. Was it stealing information and creative works? Was it being used to produce realistic deep fakes of people saying things they'd never say? And was it going to take away everyone's jobs?

And from what I knew, all of those things could be true.

Jeremy Bradshaw had founded his AI software company, Generistic, after working for a software company in Silicon Valley called Arrowfind. He'd started as an engineer, then moved into marketing. He was promoted to VP not long after.

This past year, he'd worked out an "arrangement" with his former employer regarding some proprietary technology so he could use it in his new company.

Generistic was launched with the ideal that it was going to use artificial intelligence without "stealing" from the existing works of writers, artists, and creators. I wondered how that was even possible, seeing that was pretty much what AI did—dig for info and data from sources out on the internet to put together something new.

I'd seen it at The Riverside: Bradshaw was a good-looking man, who didn't look like he spent most of his time hunkered over a computer. His wife, Amy, was young, blonde and fit. There were numerous photos of the couple in formal wear, attending events with local politicians and Silicon Valley bigwigs.

I wished I'd known the name of the older man he'd been dining with at The Riverside. I hoped the chief and Deputy Brad would find him and talk to him tomorrow. It's not like I had a lot of time to pursue this.

Nate usually gave me a goodnight call or text at 9 p.m. Now a text from him popped up on my phone. I sensed he was shaken by what we'd seen in the maze tonight.

I'm beat and need sleep. Gotta pack

Still having flashbacks from tonight

NATE HAD LOST his brother in a murder two years ago. Not like I was a coldhearted psychopath, but tonight's events would affect Nate differently than they would me.

So sorry this happened tonight, love. Sleep well. XOXO

Can't wait to see you for the dinner you're making me. Let me know what I can bring.

38

Yourself. That's enough for me 🤍

Chapter Five

Sᴜɴᴅᴀʏ ᴍᴏʀɴɪɴɢ, *October 19*

I ᴡᴏᴋᴇ up from a strange dream.

A large spider loomed down from above and began winding web strands around me, like the humongous Shelob did to Frodo in *Lord of the Rings* after Gollum led him to her lair. While I became encased in the web, the mayor's creepy clown looked on, cackling at my misfortune.

I woke up panicking at about 2 a.m. I reached down for Biga, who squeezed in closer to me. After some deep breaths and a glass of water, I was able to get back to sleep, for a few hours anyway.

At 4:30, I dragged myself out of bed and made myself some pre-coffee in the kitchen coffee maker—enough to keep me going until I could get the real stuff at the bakery. Biga burrowed into the warm quilt on the bed, unwilling to get up. I'd eventually descend on him with his crate before we left.

I sipped my coffee as I walked around the kitchen, thinking about the events of last night.

The older man in The Riverside seemed the obvious suspect in Bradshaw's death, depending on what the man claimed Bradshaw had done.

If Kirk and Elana had seen the Bradshaws socially, they must have known them at least somewhat well. I wanted to chat with my best friend's husband today.

Despite its weakness, the watery pre-coffee must have done something for me. My thoughts were coming together as I thought about what I'd research. I needed to ping the chief and tell him about Bradshaw's connection to Kirk.

I hurried into the bakery that Sunday with Biga's crate, shivering in the cold.

After setting him up in his pen, I put on my apron and went to check my harvest loaves in the proofer. The smell wafting out wrapped around me like an old, treasured blanket—pure coziness and comfort. The scent was rich and earthy. I couldn't wait to smell them baking.

It was still the weekend, so Beck came in the back door a little before six, her nose red from the cold. She had a tote with her cake tools and utensils with her. When she had a few spare minutes, or after work tonight, she'd probably work on Reggie's cake.

I wondered if she already knew about the murder from her connection via her husband Sam, who got the lowdown on police business from his best friend, Deputy Brad Castro.

"Good morning, Gracie." She nodded in my direction, but without her usual cheeriness. "I heard you were out late."

"A little late, yes," I said, as I went to the fridge to pull out the tub of cinnamon roll dough. "So you heard?"

"I knew that maze was a bad thing," she said with raised eyebrows and a disapproving look as she put on her apron and went to wash her hands. "It's not even open yet and there's been a murder."

"It might have just been a convenient spot to leave the body," I said as I dumped the dough out on the metal table and began rolling it out. "I don't think it was anything about the maze itself." I remembered my dream about the giant spider and the leering clown, and I shivered.

Beck set out a pan of tart shells and began filling them with spiced pumpkin.

"I'm staying far away from that place," Beck said emphatically. "I do have to pass it when I take the cake over to Reggie on Friday, but that's *it*." She crossed her hands in front of her like a baseball umpire calling a player safe on base.

"How's the cake going?" I asked her brightly to change the subject.

She beamed. "I'm working on the decorations for the top. Do you want to see Reggie and his friends on the park bench? I might have stayed up a little too late last night," she said with a sheepish smile that turned into a yawn.

She went to her tote and brought out a plastic container. She took the top off and brought it over to me.

Inside was a small, carefully crafted bench, textured with wood grain and grey weathered spots. She sat it down on the table and took out the five boys, who were formed in various squirmy, animated positions. They were made of white modeling chocolate and painted, but their movements looked lifelike. Like they could scamper off the bench into corners of the bakery at any minute. I bent down and inspected the figures with admiration. I looked up at Beck.

She was looking at her creation with a combination of satisfaction and some critical inspection.

"These are incredible."

"I texted a photo of them to Reggie last night." She took in a breath of excitement. "He likes them a lot."

"Of course he does," I said, giving her a high five.

She carefully took the figures off the bench and placed them back in the box, then set the bench into another small, lidded container.

As I watched Beck lovingly place her creations back in her tote bag, I thought about her journey with baking. Since I'd hired her three years ago, Beck had become an indispensable assistant manager. She'd attended to her duties in the back room conscientiously.

But I knew those duties didn't bring her the same joy as creating things like this.

I had a sense that things would change in the next few months as Beck, hopefully, realized her dream of starting a family. There was another person on staff who was continuing to show management potential and was already stepping up to it easily and naturally.

I would need to monitor this situation carefully, with some tact and grace.

I went up front and set out The Laughing Loaf Joke of the Day. I'd keep it light, since we were dealing with a new murder.

My favorite jokes were ones that made customers think as they waited in line. And maybe caught them off guard.

I laughed to myself as I put this one out on the stand:

Laughing Loaf Joke of the Day
*I was going to tell you a joke about time travel—
but you didn't like it.*

WE OPENED at 8 a.m. to a small group of River Grovians waiting outside, their frozen breath drifting up in puffs. Tristan Conway, a former Chili Cookoff winner, was there with his wife Kira and their toddler son, Rowan, who was firmly strapped into his stroller but looked like he had no intention of staying there.

On weekdays, Maeve was the door person. She loved manning the front door at opening, excited to release the chaos that poured in. Today, I was the one to flip our Laughing Loaf sign to OPEN—where our happy anthropomorphic loaf grinned, his eyes opened wide and ready to welcome everyone.

"Good morning, everyone!" I stepped back and let the small group in.

As Rowan rolled by in his stroller, I leaned toward Tristan and Kira. "Biga's here today, in his pen. I can take Rowan back later if he wants to see him."

Kira, a serious young woman who managed an accounting department, brightened. "Gracie, he would love that."

I went back to man the front counter, a few feet away from Rose who had the espresso machine warmed up and ready to go. Beck was in the back room singing along to music as she worked. It was such a contrast to the fear and discord of last night's murder scene, I almost cried. This bakery was my antidote.

A man in jeans and a leather jacket came in with his daughter. I recognized them immediately. One of Beck's older brothers, Devin. His daughter Nevaeh, about four years old, was pressing her face against the display case window, eyeing the items inside with awe.

I poked my head into the back room.

"Devin and Nevaeh are here, Beck!"

Beck came up front and immediately began asking her niece what she'd like today.

"What brings you in this morning?" I asked Devin at the counter.

He smiled and looked over at Nevaeh, whose eyes were fastened on the cinnamon roll Beck was retrieving for her from the display case.

"I missed my little sister," he said, shooting a look over at Beck, who was securing the cinnamon roll in a clam shell package. "I know Beck gets upset when something bad happens in town," he said, lowering his voice. "Like last night." He raised his eyebrows.

I smiled and continued in a lower voice. "She's excited about her cake project for Reggie, so that helps."

Devin frowned. "I did hear she was making cakes now. But the family knows she'd be happier staying home with kids."

The comment immediately activated my protective instincts, which were strong where Beck was concerned. *How do* you *know what she wants?* I tried to avoid glaring at the young man.

"Why can't she do both?" I shot him a challenging look.

Devin did a slight eye roll and grunted dismissively. I was sure most of Beck's family thought of me as a crazy outsider, filling Beck's ears with subversive ideas. I wanted Beck to be able to make up her own mind about what she wanted.

"Yeah. Why don't you give me a latte with 2% milk and an apple juice for Nevaeh."

"Sure thing." I smiled as cheerfully as I could and entered the order into our point-of-sale system. He took out his credit card and tapped it on the console.

"Thanks, Devin. Your order should be at the pickup window in just a few minutes." I smiled and watched Beck circumvent our process and come around the counter to give the cinnamon roll box to Neveah. She lifted up her niece, giving her a big hug and pressing her cheek to the little girl's. She whispered something to the girl, who scrunched up her face and giggled.

Once his coffee was ready, Devin and Neveah left to go out into the cold.

Tristan, Kira, and Rowan had settled in at a table near the window. Still in his stroller, Rowan was reaching for the basket of apples. Once the line died down a bit, I'd take him back to see Biga.

But the line grew, as more River Grovians came in for their Sunday coffee and pastries.

During the week, we got the commuters, River Grovians rushing in to pick up coffee so they could hit the road for jobs in Silicon Valley. But on Saturday and Sunday, people strolled in, sometimes with their dogs, many times with their kids. They were relaxed and conversational and the noise in the dining area was congenial and lighthearted.

Today from the comments I heard, not everyone had heard of the murder, and unfortunately my bakery might be where they first heard about it.

"Gracie, I heard something happened at the maze last night," Annie Morton said as she came up to order, glancing back at Eric and Pixie, their giant Irish wolfhound, who were huddled together out front at a table. Probably good that Pixie was outside, since Biga and the big dog often sensed each other's presence through some form of dog communication, probably scent, and riled each other up, even when they were in separate rooms.

At this point, I didn't feel like repeating my story of being in the maze last night.

I nodded as I entered her order into the system. "Unfortunately, a body was found in the maze. I don't have any more details. I'm hoping the chief will make some kind of statement today."

Annie leaned in and gave me a suspicious sideways look. "Tell me the truth, Gracie. You're usually at *lot* more in the know about these things."

I held up my hand. "I swear, Annie. I don't know much about it. Even if I had opinions about what happened, it wouldn't be right for me to say."

Annie raised an eyebrow. "Aha! So you *do* know. Well, I will wait to hear what the scoop is. You don't think anyone else in River Grove is in danger, do you?" She scrutinized my face.

"The victim wasn't from River Grove. Based on what I know, it sounds like it was a personal disagreement, and we're safe."

A look of relief settled in on Annie's face.

"Fine. That's as good as I'm going to get right now." She smiled. "Thanks, Gracie." She went over to the pickup station to wait for her drinks.

When the line got shorter, I poked my head into the back room, where Beck was taking a tray of pumpkin tarts out of the oven.

"Can you come up and take the counter in just a few

minutes? I promised Rowan Conway I'd take him back for a Biga visit."

"Aww. That's so sweet," she said with a smile. "As soon as I get these onto the cooling rack."

When she came out, I approached the Conways. Rowan was sitting in a booster seat. He looked up at me, his face smeared with frosting and crumbs. His curly blond hair was crusted with frosting.

"*Doghhh?*" He asked, extending a sticky hand out to me.

"Yes, Rowan. Let's go see *doghhh* now."

"Thank you, Gracie," Kira said, heaving a sigh of relief like a mom who needed a break.

I reached down for Rowan's warm sticky hand and guided him through the back room to Biga's pen.

Biga lay next to his chew toy, giving me a skeptical look as we approached the pen.

"Doghh. *Doghhhhh.*" Rowan mouth-breathed in quiet awe. He clapped his hands together gleefully. Before I could catch him, he extended a sticky hand through the bars of the pen.

Biga was right there. He must have seen the crumbs and frosting. He began licking Rowan's hand excitedly. What luck. This human dog toy had found his way to him.

Rowan giggled as the dog's tongue tickled his hands.

I pulled Rowan back and lifted him up.

"No *doghhh*. He can't behave himself. Wash hands." We went to the sink, and I squirted soap on the toddler's hands, rubbed them together, and rinsed them off.

Rowan was still looking in Biga's direction, moaning *dooooogghhhh* mournfully as I carried him back into the dining area to his parents.

"Biga got a little too friendly," I told Kira. "So I scrubbed Rowan's hands."

"You really love dogs, don't you, Rowan?" Kira took the toddler from me and hugged him with a warm smile.

You and me both, Rowan.

Whew. Kira had a packet of wipes at the ready and began the process of de-stickifying the boy's face and even his neck, where cinnamon roll crumbs had lodged in the folds.

By the time I'd gotten back behind the counter, the chief was standing in line scrolling on his phone. Bags drooped under his eyes and he hadn't shaved. I was sure he'd been up late dealing with last night's murder.

"Good morning, Dave."

"Drip coffee and lots of it," he said in a thin voice. "It's going to be a hell of a day."

"Any news on the murder?"

He rubbed his forehead. "Not yet. I'm just about to head to The Riverside to talk to Reggie and go over last night's credit card statements. Thanks for the details and descriptions you gave us last night. That should help."

"No problem." I went to get the largest to-go cup we had and filled it with drip coffee. I topped it with a lid. "I did a little research on Jeremy Bradshaw last night, by the way," I said, lowering my voice as I handed him the cup. "His company is the new kid on the block when it comes to artificial intelligence technology. Just a heads up, his murder will be a big deal in the local news."

The chief groaned and raised his tired eyes to the sky. "Wonderful."

He grunted and turned to leave.

By ten, customers were settled into seats in the dining area and at the tables out front. A couple leaned over a backgammon game, sipping coffee. Families chattered as they ate their pastries. With the slower pace of the weekend, the line had died down, and it looked like we'd now get a break.

Rose drifted over from the espresso machine. She looked sleepy, though her makeup techniques probably helped disguise that this morning. The cat-eye liner on her eyelids gave her a perky look.

"How do you do it, Gracie?" She moaned. "You come in earlier than I do."

"Coffee. My big secret. Don't tell anybody." I raised an eyebrow archly as I refreshed the stack of clam shell containers from under the counter. "I stayed up late googling last night's victim. Probably not the best idea for a good night's sleep."

"Only a few people have even asked about the murder," she said, stifling a yawn. She'd been with us when we found Jeremy Bradshaw, so she probably hadn't slept well either.

"The guy was well known in Silicon Valley, so the news is going to get around real quick."

And it did. After Elise and Daisy opened up the lunch line, customers coming in began asking about the murder. An article had come out in the *Mercury News*, which got the attention of anyone with Silicon Valley connections. But for most River Grove old timers, Bradshaw's name meant nothing.

Though, of course, the Schiffers had known Jeremy.

After lunch, Kirk and Elana came in for coffee. Beck was covering the front for me at that time, as I shaped loaves.

She poked her head into the back room with a cheery smile.

"Elana and Kirk are at the counter. They want to talk to you."

I quickly washed the dough off my hands and went up front.

Kirk's eyes were bloodshot and his normally well-coiffed hair looked oily and droopy this morning. Elana looked unusually pale.

"Elana told me about Jeremy Bradshaw," Kirk said weakly. "When can we talk, Gracie?"

Chapter Six

Sᴜɴᴅᴀʏ, *October 19*

Lᴏᴏᴋɪɴɢ at the crowd in the bakery and taking into account my schedule, I could give my friend and her husband ten minutes.

I steered them to a recently vacated table to one side of the busy dining area.

Kirk, being the busy CEO of BlueSoft, a software company in Santa Cruz, got to the point right away. He rubbed his eyes and blinked.

"Gracie, tell me about the circumstances of Jeremy's death."

I repeated the story of finding the man's body, then the lead-up to it: the conversation Nate and I overhead in The Riverside.

Kirk sat up in his chair, ready to engage.

"Describe the older man for me." He folded his hands and looked across at me expectantly.

"In his fifties, I think," I said, picturing him again. "Salt and pepper hair. Tall and lean. Close to Nate's height. Brown eyes, I think. He was wearing a Tampa Bay Buccaneers sweatshirt under his jacket."

Kirk lowered his head then looked up at me, a puzzled look on his face.

"Did he have an accent?"

I thought about this. "Maybe a trace of a southern accent."

"Huh." Kirk sat back in his chair, his forefinger on his chin. "That sounds like Steve Rawlins. He's legal counsel for Arrowfind, a search engine company over in Sunnyvale. I only happened to know him because he did some legal work on contract for BlueSoft right when we started out—that was before he joined Arrowfind."

Did everyone in Silicon Valley know each other? Everyone I'd met in tech seemed to have some connection, old or new, with everyone else. Maybe it was because people changed jobs so often in tech.

I'd done my googling last night, but I still didn't have a good feel for who Jeremy Bradshaw was. I hoped Kirk could give me some insight.

"Tell me a little more about Jeremy. And his AI company."

"Real smart guy. He saw an opportunity in artificial intelligence and predicted a while ago it was going to take off. Arrowfind incorporates some AI technology in their system, but Jeremy decided to invent his own. There was some talk of him poaching from his employer's staff, but I know Jeremy. He'd never do something like that. He said he wanted to run a tech company with ethics."

Elana looked to me, then Kirk. The sour expression on her face as Kirk talked made me think she had her own opinions about Jeremy.

Hmmm. A tech company with morals. Maybe that was why Jeremy had promoted his AI company as the first "honest" AI company. Was it true?

"He felt like AI should automate tedious work that people didn't want to do, so they could be free to create and use more of their brain. Do you realize people only use ten percent of their brain? Jeremy wanted to free people up to use more."

I'd heard that ten percent figure was a myth, but the truth was I had ten minutes here and I needed to pick my battles. I wanted information from Kirk and Elana.

"But eliminating tedious work," I said, relying on the info I'd been reading about Silicon Valley layoffs, "doesn't that also eliminate jobs for a lot of people?"

Kirk gave me a look that bordered on dismissive. "Gracie, those people will find other work. Work that is more satisfying. It will bring change. That's true, but it's more of an adjustment. The job market will eventually even out as people find new jobs. This happens with any innovation."

Elana took a sip of her coffee. She wasn't nodding in agreement.

"Jeremy wanted to take the sinister quality out of AI. Promote it, give it an easy-to-use interface and package it as a virtual assistant," Kirk said. "He believed it didn't have to steal from copyrighted material."

"But isn't that what it does?" I asked, as I saw Beck waving at me, a look of concern on her face. The dining area was filling up, and a line was forming at the counter.

"I've got to get back to work," I said to both my friends at the table as I stood up. "I'd like to talk to you more about this. Let me know if some night soon works for you."

Elana perked up for the first time. "Let's do that, Gracie. Kirk makes a brisket in the smoker that's really good. I know Nate's out of town this week—let me know what night works for you."

"This sounds like something Nate would hate to miss, though. Why don't we wait for when he's back from Oregon?"

Kirk stood up, smoothing his golf shirt over his abs. He flashed a beaming, naively full-of-himself smile.

"Not to brag, Gracie, but my brisket's incredible."

AFTER KIRK AND ELANA LEFT, I sighed and found myself wanting more information on Jeremy Bradshaw. I felt unsatisfied, as if I didn't have a true picture of who this man had been. Was he someone trying to bring honesty and safety to AI? Or was he just a tech bro with a marketing message he knew people wanted to hear?

I also wanted to hear Elana's opinion of Jeremy Bradshaw. When it came to gossip, Elana was truly hooked up to the pipeline. I wondered how much—and what—she knew about Jeremy.

After the line at the counter died down, I went back to do some quick folds on my sourdough loaves. It was looking and smelling perfect for this stage in the rise. If I somehow lost my sight or my hearing, I could make really good sourdough almost entirely based on smell.

After folding, I filled a tray with the scones and cinnamon rolls on the cooling racks and took them up front to replenish the display case.

Rose was at the espresso machine.

"How are you doing, Rose?" I asked after I'd loaded up the case. "Any sleep last night?"

"I feel guilty saying so, but I slept pretty well," she said, as she pulled an espresso drink to accompany a lunch order.

"I've been working so hard this week on the makeup and costumes for the maze. I went to bed and fell asleep in my clothes." She laughed. "But I did take a shower this morning, just so you know."

Rose had been doing a lot for the maze this week. Though she was in her element and loved it, I saw the effects of her late nights on her face every morning she came in. She didn't get a break between The Laughing Loaf and the maze. She was downing coffee almost as fast as I was. I mentally calculated tomorrow's staff coverage.

"After you do your cleanup and your part of the prep this afternoon, feel free to leave, Rose. Maeve's agreed to come in earlier tomorrow morning, so take some time to sleep in. Why don't you come in at 7?"

A look of relief crossed Rose's face.

"Thank you, Gracie. I appreciate that."

The dining area was lively this Sunday, full of families and a few teenagers who'd stopped by on their way from marching band practice at River Grove High. They all seemed happy to gab, sip their coffee drinks and finish off their pastries at a leisurely pace.

A uniquely River Grove phenomenon was happening that I loved to observe in the bakery: adults turned to chat with teenagers. Teenagers got down on their knees and played with the toddlers of young families camped out at their tables. Grandmas held other people's babies. People who would be strangers anywhere else struck up conversations between tables.

It was a delightful, intergenerational cross pollination that happened in my small town. In the face of last night's brutal murder, it made me feel really good about my town.

After lunch service ended, Daisy and Elise began cleaning up and returning bread and sandwich fixings to the back room. The two hadn't been involved with the maze at all, and they continued an upbeat conversation with some of the students who'd been working on it, who were hanging out near the counter.

But the events of last night were weighing on me. I needed to get out for just a few minutes of quiet.

I went up front to tell Beck and Rose, then headed into Biga's pen to put on his leash for a walk.

The back room was warm, so as soon as Biga and I headed for the alley, the brisk fall air hit me with a shot of energy. I quickened my step, which was fine with Biga. He was overjoyed to be let loose from his pen.

We headed for the trail that ran along the San Luciano River, and I felt the cold seep through my coat as we entered the thick tree cover overhead. We hadn't gotten the winter rains yet, so the river was looking a bit thin as it tumbled over exposed rocks.

As Biga scampered over to a clump of weeds by the side of the trail, I felt my phone vibrate and pulled it out of my pocket.

It was Elana. I pressed to take the call.

"Hey, what's up, my friend?"

"Just FYI," Elana said with a groan. "You did not get the full story from Kirk at the bakery this morning."

"I kinda guessed that by the way you looked at me after nearly everything Kirk said about Jeremy."

Elana sighed heavily. "So Kirk had this bromance with Jeremy. He was impressed by Jeremy and all that he's done with Generistic. He could do no wrong in Kirk's eyes. He wanted to *be* Jeremy."

I kept walking, though every ten steps, Biga found a new watering spot, so it was slow going.

"Give me the lowdown. Tell me what you couldn't say when Kirk was there."

"*First* of all," my friend launched off in the tone of a gossip columnist, "Jeremy had a reputation for . . . shall we say, 'being a ladies' man.'"

"He cheated on his wife," I interpreted for her.

"Well, that's what I heard anyway. I heard about it from the wife of one of Kirk's VPs. She saw Jeremy with a woman who was not his wife at a show in New Orleans this year. He appeared to be giving her mouth-to-mouth resuscitation."

"Whoa. So he was definitely on the prowl."

Elana continued. "Also, I don't think his artificial intelligence company is more ethical than any other AI company. He was trying to say the right words to lure in non techie people who are distrustful of AI."

Biga saw a bird take off from a nearby branch and began barking at it.

"I'd figured that was probably the case," I said as I pulled Biga back and distracted him with a treat. "Kirk seemed very convinced, though."

Another heavy sigh from Elana. "Yeah. Well, he's drunk a gallon of the Kool-Aid."

I thought about the altercation between the older man and Jeremy in The Riverside.

"Do you think somebody killed Jeremy because of his womanizing ways? I mean, I don't know if lying about his AI product would motivate someone to kill. Could he have hit on the wrong man's wife? Like, say, Steve Rawlins's wife."

"That could have been it," Elana said. "Or maybe someone else's. It's not like that would be the first time, from what I heard."

"Well, this gives me some idea of how to proceed . . . *if* I were going to try to solve this."

Elana snorted.

"Come on, girl, are you obligated by law to say that? You *always* end up working on the case." She paused. "I'm not happy that this happened. I feel for his wife and kids. I want to see this solved. And if Jeremy's wrongdoings are exposed, I'd be happy, too. Especially if it helps Kirk see the truth about the man."

"That's going to cost you extra," I smirked, as I turned around on the path and started heading back toward the bakery. Biga was not thrilled with this choice. "Keep me posted if you think about anything else that might have been going on with Jeremy."

After hanging up, I sped up to a run to give Biga a little cardio burst. Within a few minutes, we were at the back steps, satisfyingly breathless.

Beck, Rose, and I left for the day after finishing off cleaning and prep. I wrapped up a loaf of fresh sourdough, still warm, to take to Nate's.

Biga voluntarily crawled into his crate, and I locked up after everyone was out. thick

After a quick shower and settling Biga in with my dad at home, I left for dinner at Nate's.

He opened the front door wearing an apron, his hair tied back in a ponytail, and pulled me into a hug.

"Mmmm, you smell *buttery*," he said, after he finished it off with a kiss.

"That's the brioche. We're baking more of it, since everyone wants it for their sandwiches at lunch."

I followed Nate to the kitchen, where something was boiling in a big pot on the stove.

"It's pasta tonight. Bucatini marinara and roasted green beans. I hope you like it."

"I knew you were a good cook, so tell me how come you haven't cooked more meals for me?" I said, curious, as I poked my nose into the kitchen and saw thick strands of bucatini swirling in a large pot. A rich, meaty ragu bubbled in a smaller pot.

Bucatini is like spaghetti, but with a hole running through the middle. When you combine it with a sauce, you not only get the sauce on top of the pasta, you also get it filling the inside, making every bite saucy and flavorful.

He began stirring the pot, glancing at the timer.

"I don't take the time to do it for myself, and I'm often eating in the photo studio. Also . . . I'm a perfectionist."

"You can't be serious. You, a *perfectionist?*"

He grinned at me. "I have to clear my schedule to make sure I have time to prepare. And, of course, the planets have to be aligned."

"Then this will be amazing, I'm sure," I said, giving him a kiss on the cheek. "I brought sourdough I baked today. Still warm. Do you want garlic bread?"

"Are you kidding me?" Nate's blue eyes lit up. "Hell, yes."

I found a cutting board from a cupboard below the counter then pulled a well-maintained serrated knife from the knife block and began slicing the loaf.

"Garlic might help," he said with a chuckle, unceremoniously tossing a bulb onto the counter in front of me before he went back to stirring the sauce on the stove.

I opened his neatly organized utensil drawer and pulled out a garlic press, then peeled some garlic cloves and began squeezing them, scraping out the pulp into a small bowl.

I spread butter on the slices then topped that with the

minced garlic. Then I wrapped the slices in aluminum foil. I turned on the oven to 325 degrees Fahrenheit and set bundle inside to warm up and create that delicious melding of butter and garlic.

"I'm leaving at 6:15 tomorrow morning, so I can get ahead of the traffic heading north," Nate said. "Could I stop by on my way out of town for a cappuccino? And maybe a scone."

I turned to dump the papery garlic skins into the sink. "I think we can manage it. For a small *fee*."

He turned around and pulled an errant curl gently back from my face and gave me a long, slow kiss on the lips.

"Fortunately, I accept that form of payment," I said with a satisfied sigh.

We sat down to eat, and I remembered the good thing about eating dinner here and not at my own house: no Biga under the table begging for a handout. It felt so civilized.

I twirled the bucatini on my fork. It was heavier than spaghetti. After a bite, I was convinced this was a turbocharged version of pasta, and I vowed to eat this instead from now on. The sauce hidden inside the noodles gave me an extra punch of flavor.

"This might be the best pasta I've ever had." I took another bite and savored it. "It's like the pasta equivalent of stuffed pizza. You are going to make this again, right? For *me*?"

Nate blushed just a bit at the compliment.

"Of course. I need you to eat it, too, so I don't eat all of it myself."

He was more subdued tonight. I thought of how shaken he'd looked after the maze experience and finding Bradshaw.

"How are you feeling today?"

Nate shrugged as he picked up a slice of hot garlic bread. "I'm not going to lie. That was intense. I am hoping that's the last dead body I find. I had maze flashbacks in my dreams."

I nodded. "Me, too. It's hard enough finding a body. Worse when you're trapped with it until you figure out how to get out."

"Did you find out anything more about the guy?"

"Maybe too much. Kirk and Elana came by the bakery this morning and wanted to ask about Bradshaw. Kirk knew him well. Maybe even idolized him, a little too much, for his work in AI." I told him what Kirk had said, and then about Elana's insights, which were a little gossipy but at least based on firsthand knowledge and worth looking into.

"So maybe that's what the older man in The Riverside was upset about."

"It could be. Kirk said he knew the guy—Steve Rawlins. He works as legal counsel at Arrowfind in Sunnyvale."

"What happens next then?"

"I passed my info on to the chief. So we'll see if that helps his investigation. The chief's not really in his element. He's not a Silicon Valley guy."

"And you worked in tech." He gave me a searching look. "So you know a lot more about how that world works."

Was he digging to find out if I was going to get involved in the case? Nate had had his issues with me getting involved in cases and putting myself in danger. He'd brought it up in his therapy sessions, as a matter of fact. He'd lost his parents to a plane crash and his brother to murder. He didn't want to lose me.

"I do know more about the tech world than the chief." I nodded and watched marinara sauce ooze out of the buca-tini noodles on my plate, a beautiful sight. "But I'm not sure if I'll get involved. Depends on what I have going at the bakery. And how intrigued I am by the case."

"Of course it does," Nate said with a smile. "I've seen it. You begin collecting the facts. You sort through them like I sort through my laundry. You cycle through possibilities in your head. It starts to take up more and more of your thoughts as you try to fill in the pieces."

He spooned shaved Parmigiano Reggiano over his bucatini and continued.

"Then you're hooked. I have literally sat across from you at dinner and seen the wheels turning in your head."

"I've got to do *something* with my time. I can't just sit around moping because my boyfriend's away. You'll be up in Oregon for your photo shoot all week." I threw a dramatic hand to my brow.

"Why don't you get outside? Take a walk? This is your favorite season," he said, while twirling pasta strands around his fork. "You spend a lot of time inside at the bakery."

Nate was a sportsman, someone who felt out of sorts if he didn't get out and exercise on any given day, but still it was a strange comment.

I set down my fork and cleared my throat. "Do I look like I need exercise?"

"I'm just saying it's healthy to get outside and move sometimes, that's all," he said, calmly twirling his pasta on his fork.

I sighed and narrowed my eyes at him. "I spend most of my time inside, but you *do* know I'm constantly moving at the bakery, right? Going up front to work the counter, going to the back room, kneading dough, cleaning tables, and moving supplies in and out of the storeroom." I left out sitting in front of my computer because that wasn't going to help my case.

"Gracie, I am just saying it might be good for you to get outside. Take a break and breathe some fresh air. Get your heart rate up. Take Biga for more walks."

Nate had only ever been supportive and loving to me, so I didn't think this was a slam on my physical appearance. But for some reason, it felt like it. Honestly, I was a sedentary person just like my parents had been.

He cleared his plate and gave me an endearing smile, oblivious to the effect his comment had had on me.

He reached for my hand. "If you look into the case this week, which I know you will do, I hope you solve this. I want to know what really happened to the guy. You're good at this, Gracie. And even though I worry, and always will, I know you can take care of yourself."

After eating, I helped him clear the table and load the dishwasher.

Then we adjourned to his sofa to indulge in the kind of activity we wouldn't feel comfortable doing at my house, across from my dad in his recliner.

Chapter Seven

Monday, *October 20*

THE NEXT MORNING, I got up early, determined to fit in some research online at the bakery.

Biga wasn't thrilled at getting up earlier, but he reluctantly went along for the ride, giving me a very nasty look as he crawled into his crate.

As soon as I got in the door, I started an upbeat playlist on the sound system. I rolled up and cut two trays' worth of cinnamon rolls. I let them rise while I sat down at my computer and googled Steve Rawlins.

The man appeared on the screen wearing a San Francisco 49ers t-shirt in front of Levi Stadium in Santa Clara. Steve Rawlins had an approachable, friendly smile. He looked casual, sports-minded, and down to earth.

He presented well online. He'd been at his position at Arrowfind for eight years, during which he'd risen from corporate legal staff to head legal counsel. He volunteered for a group that worked with disabled youth, and he'd also coached his daughter's soccer team to a championship.

Family pictures showed him with a willowy, blonde wife and two teenaged children. His daughter was tall and athletic, and looked college age. His son, a few years younger, used a wheelchair.

There was a photo of Steve Rawlins and Jeremy Bradshaw together on what looked like a palm tree–lined beach with their families, all wearing leis around their necks.

It struck me that these people looked genuinely happy and comfortable with each other. This wasn't a staged picture to show some sort of alliance for business purposes. It looked like a group of people who got together often and knew each other well. Like family.

At 6 a.m., Beck came in, followed by Maeve. I ended my search, copying a few links for later. I needed to get to work.

"G'morning, Gracie!" Beck called as she set down a basket of fresh eggs from her chickens. She was cheery, but there were circles under her eyes, and I suspected she'd been up late working on her cake for Reggie.

Maeve put on her apron, then went over to peer into the proofer.

"Ah, the usual this morning. Those brioche loaves are looking good. I talked to Rafal this weekend about switching to your recipe. It's better than what we've got. And with all the batches we've been making for the lunch line, I could make it in my sleep."

"I have no problem with that." I nodded, as I pushed my office chair in and prepared to get back to work. "Maybe you could show me how you and Rafal do your rye loaves."

"They're good," she said with a smile. "They might be a nice addition to our sandwich offerings."

After the cinnamon rolls came out of the oven, I set two aside for Nate for when he stopped by. They smelled especially good this morning, with the blend of cinnamon and caramel. After I let them cool, I put them in a paper tote, along with a small packet of wet wipes. My fastidious boyfriend would not want to sully his steering wheel with stickiness.

Then I heard a knock coming from the front door.

"Wonder who that could be." Maeve laughed over the noise of the industrial mixer as I ran to the front to let Nate in.

I waved him over to the espresso machine.

He had that fresh-scrubbed look, his just shaved face pink from the cold, his hair still curly and damp from the shower. He smelled like soap and freshly washed clothes.

He gave me a kiss on the cheek.

"Breakfast's packed and ready," I told him. "Just about to make your cappuccino, so it's nice and hot."

He followed me to the espresso machine and watched as I made his drink.

"I love the cold mornings, right before I take off on a trip," he said, setting down his backpack and leaning on the counter. "The thrill of hitting the road to explore a new place. Wish you could come with me."

Nate was like the creatures he loved; a bird migrating and returning to the place he'd left. Someday I would come with him on one of his trips. Right now, I was happy for him to have this break from civilization and to be with the birds and wildlife he felt more comfortable with. He and his camera came back full of all he'd seen, all the moments captured that he then got to review, cull, tweak, and share in his photos.

"I'm craving good bird pictures," I said, setting his drink

down in front of him. It wasn't like I was a huge bird fan, just a huge Nate fan. I loved the joy in his voice as he described what he'd seen. I liked to listen to the detailed explanations of the creatures he'd tracked, how they interacted with their environment, and how he described their small lives as part of a huge and complex system of land and living things. I could not get enough of the thrill in his quiet voice, the awe and fascination in his words.

"I'll send some tomorrow." He bent over the counter and gave me a kiss before he left. "You'll let me know when you find out more about the case, won't you?"

He didn't say be careful. The unspoken words were still there, and those words were right. The further I got into investigating the murder in the maze, the more I'd see it: I absolutely did need to be careful.

BECK SPENT her lunch break working on Reggie's birthday cake.

Of course, while she worked in her corner of the back room on her intricate cake topper diorama, she also supervised a delivery of flour and sugar headed for our storeroom, checked in with Maeve about the timing of her bakes, and fielded questions from Daisy and Elise on restocking items for the sandwich line.

"I am *so* close to being done, I just want to keep going," she said, a growl of frustration in her voice. "It almost hurts to not be able to finish now. I may have to set this aside and stay late tonight."

It was beyond me how Beck could continue with such focus on perfecting the details of her cake topper while noise and activity swirled around her.

Growing up in a house with five noisy brothers probably had something to do with it.

"Nate's away, so I may stay late myself to work on some accounting reports--which is hard to do with lots of people around."

"Then it'll be like the old days when it was just the two of us." She beamed with excitement.

The old days really weren't that old. Up until a year ago, it was just me and Beck, with Chloe Westerman and her friend, Aiden, filling in during busy times.

Looking back, I should have hired more staff earlier. The bakery had become profitable quickly. We'd both worked hard, and, as the only employees, the two of us had to do *everything*. It had been an intense learning experience.

"Why don't we order dinner from The Riverside and work late?" I suggested. "With Nate out of town, I can work until 8:30. Does that work for you?"

Beck looked up excitedly. "That'll give me time to finish the cake topper. I'll let Sam know."

At 2 p.m. our lunch crew shut down the sandwich line. They brought meats and toppings back to the fridge and wrapped up leftover breads, naan, and flatbreads.

"Gracie, Mayor C came in to pick up sandwiches," Daisy said. "She wants to talk when you get a chance."

I pulled my phone out of my apron pocket and texted her.

> I can talk after 2:30

> Come to back door

> I'll come out with Biga. Short walk?

. . .

BIGA HAD BEEN WAITING in his pen patiently (well, for him), for me to take him out for fresh air and pee time.

Twenty minutes later, the mayor knocked on the back door. I saw her face through the back window and tried to gauge her mood. She was frowning, a common look for her, so that didn't give me a lot of information. She could be upset about the quality of the sandwich she'd received today, or angry we hadn't posted enough flyers for the Haunted Maze. Or she could have had a falling out with the chief.

I waved at her, then went to Biga's pen to clip on his leash. I slid on my down jacket.

Biga and I met her at the back door.

"Gracie, let's head over to the river trail," she said tersely.

Biga looked up at me, then the mayor, with an excited look as we headed across the alley to the trail. Biga had his favorites. He loved Reggie and adored Nate. But he hadn't had much exposure to Mayor C. Since anyone willing to go on a walk with him was an instant friend, he looked up at her, grinning goofily, his tongue hanging out.

"Uh, hey there . . . *Biga*," the mayor, normally a cat person, said haltingly as she bent down toward him, not sure she actually wanted to touch him.

As we headed onto the shaded trail, I shivered. I heard the river rushing over the rocks a few yards away. It had been the soundtrack for my time in River Grove. It was always there. We couldn't see it, but we could hear it.

She started in, her voice gravelly. "Gracie, we've got a problem. Gordon and I are very concerned. Ticket sales on the website took a huge drop today. We've sold *two*."

"But it's only Monday. Everyone's back to work or school after the weekend. That's normal."

The mayor sighed, a skeptical look in her eyes. "I've got to be realistic. The maze murder will hurt us. Apparently, this Jeremy Bradshaw was well known in the tech world, about to launch some new AI company. He was killed *in* our maze. The message is, 'River Grove is a dangerous place. The maze is not safe.'"

I thought about this as Biga stopped to water a seedling just off the trail. "Granted, these are River Grovians. Judging by the conversation in the bakery today, there wasn't a lot of interest in the murder. Most people thought it was a Silicon Valley problem and didn't concern them. And as far as the teenagers are concerned, the maze now has more cred. It's scarier and more exciting now that there's been a murder in it."

As if on cue, two teenagers on bikes came toward us on the trail and quickly veered around us.

"Parents, though," the mayor said, her voice tense. "A few already left messages at City Hall. They have no intention of coming to the maze or letting their children go. They think it's too dangerous. After we spent time and money to set up a special area for younger kids, too."

I nodded sympathetically. "Parents want to keep their kids safe. That's the reason some of them moved here." I wanted to say this, but I didn't: *Who wants to put their kids in costumes and take them to a murder scene?*

"The chief briefed me today. He and Brad are tracking down a lead. Apparently, locals saw the man having dinner with someone at The Riverside and they had a blowout in the dining area—"

"Yeah, Nate and I were those locals," I said wearily,

wanting to pretend otherwise. I was tired of telling the story. "And I found out Kirk Schiffer knows Bradshaw."

"If the chief makes an arrest, that would help," the mayor nodded. "And if you were to look into this, Gracie, especially if it turns out this murder had *nothing* to do with River Grove and the maze, it would reassure people."

"I'm not sure what I can do that would make people feel safer. I have done some research. I'll try to get some time with the chief and touch base."

As we got deeper into the woods, the temperature dropped. Even Biga looked up at me, shivering from the cold wind as it swept past us.

"Gracie, I gotta get back." The mayor turned to me. "Gordon Dabney and I need to talk about doing some public relations for the maze."

We turned around on the trail. As the mayor and I walked in silence back toward the alley, I took in a deep breath of the brisk, fall air.

The massive, burnished redwoods and the river, sloshing over stones in its bed, carried on doing their jobs, oblivious to who had murdered whom in River Grove--and why. The trees looming high above us had been here for over a hundred years and they would continue for hundreds more.

The thought centered me somehow.

Biga and I crossed over to the alley, headed for the back door.

Then I saw activity going on next door behind Loudon's Antique Emporium. Workers, wisely wearing masks, were carrying furniture, knickknacks, old steamer trunks, and piles of old clothes out the store's back door and depositing them in the alley.

I walked over with Biga and took a look at the merchandise. As expected, the items weren't worth much. There were some cute vintage dresses Rose might be interested in. The only thing that caught my eye was a full-length mirror, with an ornate brass frame. It looked like something from the Gilded Age.

Still stinging from Nate's weird comment at dinner last night, I stood in front of the mirror, examining myself critically.

I looked at myself from a front and side view to see if I showed any signs of looking out of shape. I stood up straight, then slumped down. I turned around in the mirror, critically examining my profile, even my backside.

What the hell, Nate Berhrens.

Since we were already outside and things weren't busy at the bakery, I decided to take Biga on a short walk through downtown.

I headed for The Corner Market, a place I normally never went to, especially since our lunch service provided way better sandwiches than the wrapped ones in their refrigerator case.

The Corner Market had been run by the Delgado family for two generations. Elise Delgado, young daughter of the current owners, worked on The Laughing Loaf's lunch crew.

There weren't any big chain grocery stores in River Grove. The Corner Market filled the need as a place to pick up something for dinner or lunch without having to get in your car and leave town. The store also carried an odd assortment of impulse items and anything tourists on their way through town might need for a day at the beach.

I'd seen dogs in the market before, so I brought Biga in with me.

"Hi, Gracie," Dylan Delgado, Elise's twenty-something brother, greeted me as he unpacked bags of tortilla chips from a box. He wore a River Rats baseball cap, having played on the softball team with Nate this year. "Haven't seen you around for a while. What's up?"

Hip-hop blared on the sound system, with the bass turned up about as high as it could go.

He quickly turned down the volume.

Biga sniffed around eagerly, overcome by the scents of many forms of his favorite thing: food.

"Just busy baking. Hey, is it okay to have Biga in here with me? I'm looking for a step counter. I thought you guys might have one."

He waved dismissively. "Biga's not a problem. I think we do have some step counters. But they're the really old kind. Everyone's using their phones or those fancy digital tracking bands."

Dylan went to the back of the store, where accessories, hats and cheap sunglasses were kept on hooks on the wall. He started talking to someone who was working in the back.

"Hey, bruh. Got any step counters back there?"

I angled my head to see if this person was someone I recognized. It was a short man around forty, with overgrown dark hair. He scowled, and it looked like he'd had the expression so long it had become permanent. The man didn't look familiar.

Dylan brought back a few things and set them on the counter.

"Here's what we got," he said, as I looked through them. "They work. They're just not fancy and nobody wants 'em."

I picked out a blue one with a clip that looked like you could attach it to a belt or pocket.

"I'll take it." I handed him cash. The thing was cheap. "Thanks, Dylan."

"Good to see you, Gracie. And you, too, Biga!" Dylan turned the music back up and went back to unpacking bags of chips.

After we left the shop, I opened the package and pushed the device's tiny black start button with my fingernail. I clipped the counter to the pocket of my jeans.

Then we were off.

Just to make sure the thing worked, I walked around the block with Biga, which made him very happy. We walked past The Laughing Loaf to Key Haus, where Hans Schultz waved through the window as he put up the store's Halloween decorations.

Then we headed back to the alley.

Once I got to the bakery's back door, I checked the counter: 1,126 steps. Not bad for a short walk. I'd monitor my steps in the bakery, too.

But if I were going to get more exercise, I'd have to do better than that.

I read online that ten thousand steps was a worthy goal.

I decided I'd try to hit that amount every day until Nate got back.

Chapter Eight

Monday, *October 20*

At 5 p.m., Rose and Maeve left for the day. Rose had promised Maeve a makeup demonstration over at the maze, before she started working with maze actors on makeup and costuming.

The mayor sent out what she'd hoped was a reassuring announcement: The maze would proceed with its Friday night opening pending further developments.

The gist of her message was what I had expected: the chief had some leads, and the people involved in this murder were from Silicon Valley. Definitely *not* upright, goodhearted River Grovians. I was skeptical that this spin would reassure attendees. I also hoped she was right; we'd get to the bottom of this murder soon and then feel free to enjoy the imaginary horrors of the maze.

By 6 p.m., Beck and I had finished our prep, and I'd ordered takeout from The Riverside. A rock playlist blared from the speakers, as we busied ourselves with our respective projects.

I'd generated reports on our monthly revenue, with detail on what products were selling well. Tracking this data helped me make decisions on what to offer, and possibly what items to phase out. The point-of-sale system we added with our bakery renovation did all the data collection, which was a huge help. No big surprises here as to what was popular: Beignets, cinnamon rolls, and apple tarts were our top sellers. French toast sticks were by far our biggest seller *before* 8 a.m. Thank you, River Grove teens.

Lunch service was best on Mondays and Fridays—the days on which tech-employed River Grovians worked from home and ventured out of their remote-work caves to grab lunch. Flatbread wraps, naanini, and brioche bread were overwhelming lunch favorites, no mystery there.

While Beck leaned over the cake topper, fine-tuning the details on the molding chocolate, I moved on to what had been obsessing me for the past two days: the murder in the maze.

I did another, more detailed online search on Jeremy Bradshaw.

Multiple stories flooded the news feed, in the light of his murder.

One was an interview with his wife, Amy Bradshaw, who looked not only beautiful but really smart. She'd attended UCLA, where the couple had met.

A retrospective on his contributions to the tech industry talked about Bradshaw's desire to limit the scope of Generistic's artificial intelligence to a source of practical help, like a personal virtual assistant. And in a time where many people seemed suspicious of AI, this message was getting a lot of attention.

An opinion piece by a local newspaper debated whether Bradshaw's plans for a "better, more moral" AI were true or even possible. An accompanying article traced the history of artificial intelligence from the 1950s to now. It was interesting to me, mostly for what it could reveal about Bradshaw and what he'd been trying to do with his new company.

I must have plunged myself pretty deeply into my research, because I heard Beck's voice distantly calling my name and I realized she was laughing at me.

"Gracie! Those accounting reports must be *so* fascinating," she said with a giggle. "Can't you smell the food? Willow from The Riverside dropped it off on her way home."

Only then did I realize how hungry I was.

Beck grabbed paper plates from the storeroom, and I took the food up front. We plunked down at a table in the back of the dining area.

Beck took items out of the bags.

"Guac and chips," Beck pulled a container out and looked across at me, wearing a mock look of puzzlement. "Hmm, I don't remember ordering that for myself. Maybe there was some mistake with the order."

I snatched the container from her, laughing.

"And those new empanadas Maeve's been talking about." She took out a clamshell container. "Have you had them? They're so good. I *guess* I can share."

We laid everything out on the table and devoured it while chatting.

"The cake's going well?" I asked between loading chips up with guacamole. "He needs it for Friday, right?"

Beck nodded. "It's right on track. He gave me a lot longer on this one, and I'm learning how to use my time better. Instead of staying up all night the day before." She groaned and laughed. "I'm baking a test cake. Reggie's pastry chef told me there are cake "dummies"—foam, reusable cake layers you can use to test your design, but I haven't done four layers before. So I want to test it with real layers. I'll have the decorations ready tomorrow, put it together to test it out, then I'll bake the final layers Thursday night. I've got my schedule all set up." She finished off an empanada in two quick bites. "I'm learning to *adult,* as Maeve says."

I gave her a high five. "You've been good at that since I met you, Beck. But I know what you mean. Everybody's got something to work on in that area. Mine is dealing with Mayor C, figuring out how to stay on her good side without letting her give me more work to do."

Beck giggled. "Ha! That's good."

I wanted to ask more about her family planning time-line, but I didn't feel I could. If this were Elana, I'd feel free to ask a question like that, but Beck was my employee. If she wanted to talk about it, she could bring it up.

Funny, when I'd been a manager in tech back in Seattle, I never had more than superficial conversations with my staff. Granted most of them were men, so that might have had something to do with it.

But Beck must have felt much looser with those boundaries, since she plunged right in.

"You're gonna miss Nate this week?" Beck asked as she picked up another empanada and dipped it in sauce.

"Of course I will," I said, thinking about how much to say, then deciding I didn't need to go into too much detail. "It gives me time to do other things, though. Like think about the maze murder."

Beck sat and thought about this, then veered into an unexpected direction.

She looked at me a few times as if assessing whether she should ask.

"A few months ago, you said you had an ex. Someone who did some bad things. You said . . . he was in—" she took a deep breath "—*prison.*"

I also took a deep breath. "He is."

She searched my face for clues. "He's not like Nate at all."

"No comparison."

"Do you ever miss him?" She looked at me matter-of-factly.

I scraped at the rapidly emptying tub of guacamole with a tortilla chip.

"Sometimes I miss who I thought he was," I said with a wry smile.

Beck stopped and sat back in her seat, watching me with her bright, brown eyes as she munched on chips.

"It took a while to let go of that," I said. "But I think I have. Moving here helped a lot."

"Did he ever say he was sorry for what he did?" Beck gave me such a look of shock and sadness, I didn't quite know what to say. I don't think the words *I'm sorry* were in Ben's vocabulary. I tried to remember if I'd ever heard him say them.

"Nope."

I immediately started thinking of anything else but Ben. I didn't want to go there. Could I imagine him ever saying those words? No way in hell. How would that even make me *feel*?

"Maybe that was bad of me to ask, Gracie. But I feel sad sometimes. That must have been hard for you." She looked so earnest and thoughtful as she tilted her head and considered this that I almost cried.

"That's kind of you, Beck. Don't feel bad," I said with a smile. "I could never imagine him apologizing, and I don't expect it."

I grabbed an empanada from the takeout box, since Beck was devouring them at lightning speed.

Beck shook her head. "I'm glad your life is so much better now. You don't wish you were with Nate right now?"

"Maybe I'll go on a shoot with him someday." I thought about the times Nate had hinted that he wanted me to. "But he's doing something he loves. I'm doing what I love here at the bakery. I can't wait to hear the stories and see all his pictures."

Beck continued with that thoughtful look. "You and I are so different, Gracie. If Sam went away for a week, I'd miss him so much I don't think I could handle it."

Beck and Sam had been married shortly before I came to River Grove. There was a quiet innocence about both of them, and they loved their domestic bliss. They both pitched in around the house, worked on home improvement projects together and took pride in their small home. Their life right now was pre-kid, without any major life stressors other than the strong desire to have a child. I wondered how a child would change their lives. Maybe I was being cynical that it would disrupt their happy, devoted marriage. After all, this was Beck and Sam, not me.

After we finished with the remains of our appetizers, Beck showed me her almost-complete decorations for the top of the cake: Reggie and his friends on a bench, which was finished, then the beginnings of a hedge of shrubs that would run around the perimeter of the cake. I was surprised to see a dog with a toy in his mouth who looked a lot like my pup.

"Hey, that's Biga!" I laughed.

She grinned. "He was here when I was working on the design. I thought it would be really cute to have him on Reggie's cake. I showed Reggie, and he loved it."

"Well, the two of them *are* buddies," I said.

"I think I'll stay a little longer and finish up the hedge," she said, examining the white chocolate shrub she'd started painting as an example. "Then I'll assemble the top decorations Friday. Chef Jorge says I can do that in The Riverside's kitchen. He gave me the key to the secret kitchen entrance on the side."

"And I've got more research to do," I said, looking over at my computer. I stifled a yawn, since I had been here almost fifteen hours. "I'm going to check in with the chief tomorrow morning to see how the case is going. Mayor C is worried about the maze attendance and wants a quick end to this."

Beck gave me a thumbs-up as she turned back to her cake, and we both went off to our respective work.

Beck put on a playlist of folk rock, which was lighter and more conducive to focused work.

I went back to my seat at my computer. I decided to search for more info about Jeremy and Amy Bradshaw.

I yawned and did a quick stretch to shake myself awake. It was 7 p.m., and I was feeling the effects of a food coma.

Not long into my online search, I stumbled upon something so surprising that I had to read it twice.

I sat back in my seat, going over it again.

I was awake now.

Chapter Nine

MONDAY, October 20

Total step count for Monday: 5,215

AMY BRADSHAW HAD GROWN up in River Grove. Born and raised.

I followed the trail down a rabbit hole of links that led me to the following information.

Her parents were Thomas and Candace Muller, who, according to further googling, lived a half mile from me on Cannes Way, right off the river trail.

Twenty-five years ago, Amy had graduated from River Grove High School, where she'd been valedictorian and a star on the gymnastics team. An article in the *Santa Cruz Sentinel* featured an interview with Amy Muller and another River Grove graduate. Both of them had won the same local scholarship and would be attending UCLA that coming fall.

I opened a text file and typed in my notes. Could Amy Bradshaw's connection to River Grove have anything to do with the fact that her husband had been killed here?

It could be coincidence. But it was pretty handy that there were people related to Amy, and her husband, here in town.

I thought about who might have known Amy growing up.

Mayor C would be a year or two older than Amy. Kirk Schiffer would be right around Amy's age, if he'd be willing to talk to me about anything that wouldn't be anathema to his bromance with Jeremy.

I watched Beck smile to herself as she examined her finished cake decorations. I thought about what her brother Devin had said, that *everyone* knew all Beck wanted to do was have children and stay home with them.

My gifted assistant loved creating baked goods. I couldn't imagine her not doing this. But it was her choice to make, not mine.

"You've had fun with this. I can tell," I said, as she returned her decorations to their containers.

Her face glowed with excitement. "So much fun, Gracie. I can't believe how lucky I am to be doing this."

When she was done packing up, Beck and I walked out to our cars in the alley. We shivered in the cold damp evening as we nailed down details of tomorrow morning's bakes.

I made sure she was in her car, motor running and ready to leave. Then I got in my car and went home, ready to lay down for as long a night sleep as I could get.

I CAME in the front door to see my dad in his recliner, absorbed in a presentation on the physics concept of entropy. So absorbed, it took him a while to realize I was there.

"Hey, dad. How was your evening?"

As usual, it took him a few minutes to make the transition from theoretical physics to human conversation.

"I'm trying to come up with a short explanation of entropy for my students. They're struggling with the laws of thermodynamics. I'm trying to figure out what they're confused about."

I smiled at him affectionately. "Because it seems quite clear to you, right?"

"Yes, exactly," he said with a nod.

In the past year, my father had started offering after-hours physics tutoring for River Grove High School students. He was able to use his forty years of experience as a physics professor to help the kids as they struggled with the complex subject.

He tried his explanation out on me, and when he finished, he asked me if I understood it. I yawned through it, but in my defense, I'd had a very long day.

"Um, I guess I'm following you," I said. "But then I have some background in physics, just because of your conversations with me when I was growing up. Your students haven't had the benefit of that." I tried to picture the teens I knew from the bakery. "Have you tried asking them to repeat back to you what they *think* you said? Or even to draw it out on paper? Some might need to see it to understand it."

"Hmm. I hadn't thought about that. I might give that a try."

Twenty minutes later, after hearing another, easier-to-grasp explanation of the theory from my father, I curled up in my warm bed with Biga, who'd followed me into my room, not at all interested in physics talk.

Then I saw that Nate had texted at 9 p.m.

I texted back:

> Wanna chat?

He called me right back.

"I'm in a cabin on the Deschutes River. It's even colder than River Grove, if you can believe it."

"How cold?"

"20 degrees."

"Okay, you win," I said. "What creatures could possibly exist in such a freezing, inhospitable climate?"

"Now you're talking like a true Californian," he said. I felt the low rumble of his laugh even over the phone. "What was it in River Grove today? A balmy 63 degrees? I hope you remembered your sunscreen."

After he sent me a video clip of a skunk skulking suspiciously around outside his cabin, I told him about tonight's research and about discovering Amy Bradshaw's River Grove roots.

"So there *is* a local connection with Jeremy's murder?" he said.

"I'm not sure. It does give me some local contacts for asking questions. I'll talk to Mayor C tomorrow. She was a year or two ahead of Amy in school. She knows everyone and their family."

"I'm surprised you're not planning to go right to the source, Mrs. Bradshaw herself," Nate said.

That would make sense. "If her parents are still in town,

she may be spending some time with them after what happened. I'll see what I can do."

After we hung up, I decided to text the chief. If he had to do a next-of-kin notification, he might know about Amy Bradshaw's family.

> You know Bradshaw's wife grew up in River Grove?

> Way ahead of you, kiddo. I talked to her at her parents' place today.

That answered the question for me. I hoped to see Amy—or her parents—very soon.

Chapter Ten

Tuesday, *October 21*

The next morning, I downed an unsatisfying cup of weak pre-coffee, made in my ancient home drip maker, then lured Biga into his crate.

"I promise you will get at least one mid-morning W-A-L-K," I told Biga, spelling it out, because when I said the word, he assumed the walk was happening *now*.

I stepped out into the cold, damp early morning and deposited the crate in the back seat.

A few drops hit my forehead as I got into my car. This time it was condensation dripping from the trees, which often happened among the redwoods. If rain did start up today, that would not bode well for the Haunted Maze volunteers. No rain was predicted until after Halloween, but in River Grove, as well as up in Seattle, those predictions often meant absolutely nothing.

I pulled into the alley and parked, and as I got out, I felt a few drops pelting down from the actual sky.

The bakery felt warm and dry, though, as I came through with Biga's crate and a bag of clean aprons over my shoulder.

I set Biga in his pen and made him jump for his morning treat. I filled his bowl with food and went to wash my hands so I could get to work.

Beck opened the door, wedging herself in as she tried to enter carrying a large tote bag brimming with decorating supplies in one hand and a basket of eggs from her chickens in the other. I ran to hold the door open for her and took the egg basket from her hand.

"Thanks, Gracie," she said with a sigh of relief. She was pale and there were circles under her eyes. "I threw anything I thought I'd need in my bag. I did some fine-tuning on my decorations last night. I probably shouldn't have. But I was wide awake when I got home last night and wanted to keep working on it. I only stayed up till midnight. But good news! I'm all finished." She set her decorations out on her workspace one more time and looked at them with satisfaction. The hedge curving around the perimeter of the cake looked like an actual tiny shrubbery with detailed, carefully painted leaves.

"So you got, what, four hours of sleep?" I raised my eyebrows and gave her a disapproving look.

Lecturing Beck on work-life balance, when it related to one of her creative projects, wasn't going to work. When Beck entered the zone, she didn't want to leave it till she was done with her creation. She was like Michelangelo, chipping away at a block of marble until she revealed her nearly living, breathing David. Only in this case, her medium was modeling chocolate, which she'd then put on a delicious cake.

"Let me get those tart shells filled," she said with a

yawn. As she went to pull out the pans of baked shells, I rolled cinnamon roll dough into two big rectangles, then went to the stove to retrieve my pot of filling: a melted blend of brown sugar, cinnamon, butter, and caramel sauce.

"I've got some info on the maze murder. The victim's wife grew up in River Grove. Her name, before she got married, was Muller. Amy Muller."

Beck looked up from arranging apple slices in the shells. Her eyes brightened. "The Mullers. They lived down here, near downtown. They went to our church for a while. Two kids, a lot older than me. Amy babysat me and my brother Korban once, and she was super nice. But her brother Michael was a little scary."

My head popped up. "Why was he scary?"

Beck continued filling the tarts in the tray calmly. "He seemed angry all the time. Like he was swearing at us, like, under his breath or something. I mean, I didn't hear the actual words, but it just felt like he was."

I thought of the man working the back room at The Corner Market.

I moved on to attend to the bread loaves, as Beck continued with our breakfast pastries. When Maeve came in at 6 a.m., she switched the playlist to something livelier and began singing along as she checked the loaves in the proofer. Rose came in right after her, looking tired.

She took the beignet dough out of the fridge, then went up front to turn on the espresso machine.

"I was up late at the maze," Rose said. "Anyone else need coffee besides me?"

Of course, everyone called out that they did. Once we had our jolt of caffeine, conversation picked up considerably, and so did our workflow.

I set the day's joke on its stand on the counter. I was

proud of myself. It was on point, considering Mayor C's addition to the maze entrance:

Laughing Loaf Joke of the Day
Why don't monsters eat clowns?
They taste funny.

Maeve opened the door at 7:30 a.m. to a lively bunch of teens, who jostled each other to get through the door, dropped their backpacks off at tables, and raced to get in line for breakfast.

Chloe Westerman, the chief's granddaughter, got to the counter first, and she ordered for her friends, Aiden and Amelia, who called to her their last-minute additions to their orders.

"Good morning, Gracie!" Chloe said, as she glanced at the menu. "Two large chai lattes, one medium mocha with oat milk. Then two orders of French toast sticks, and one cinnamon roll."

"You working on the maze at all, Chloe?"

She shook her head. "Too many AP classes this semester, and I'm still on cheer squad. "Aiden's playing a mad scientist, though. I *have* to go and see that."

Aiden called out indignantly from the table. "Hey! I'm Dr. Frankenstein! Not just any mad scientist."

"Good luck with your classes, Chloe. I remember those crazy semesters."

"Thanks, Gracie." She turned to head for the pickup window. "Not that I'm in charge of his social schedule, but the chief says he wants to talk to you today. Just a heads up."

This was par for the course as far as his investigations. I wasn't surprised. And I did want to hear about his progress.

"Thanks, Chloe," I called after her. "I'll check in with him."

As always, I sighed with relief as the noisy horde of teenagers flooded out, on their way to River Grove High School. But once they were gone, I missed their energy and craziness just a little.

At 8 a.m., the bakery's usual suspects came in. Jake Daniels, candidate for best boss ever, picked up scones for his staff at Speed Spot Motors. Several young tech types wearing hoodies and sweatpants grabbed coffee, then settled in on laptops in our dining area.

A few minutes later, a couple in their sixties joined the line at the counter. They looked vaguely familiar, as if I'd seen them in the bakery a time or two before.

"Nice dad joke, Gracie," the man said, with an appreciative smile as he read the joke of the day. "I appreciate a good groaner when I see one," he said, chuckling.

"Thanks." I grinned. "The teens who come in every morning would disagree with you. But I enjoy them."

He looked over at the display case thoughtfully.

"We'll need one of those big pink boxes today. This is for a small crowd," the balding man with wire rimmed glasses said with a wry smile. "We've got the grandchildren with us. What would you recommend? Maybe some cinnamon rolls?"

"You've got it." I gave him a friendly smile and wondered if my instincts were correct as to who this was. By the look of the woman's eyes, she'd been crying. She waited behind him, her lips tight and her face drawn.

"I've got some kid-sized treats we keep on hand to give out to the little ones. I can throw a few of those in—some small cinnamon rolls and a few baby beignets. Anything else you'd like today?"

He leaned over and looked at the display case. "How about a couple of those tarts. The pumpkin and apple ones." He turned around to his wife. "What do you say, Candace?"

"That sounds nice," she dabbed at her eyes and nodded distractedly. "And one for Amy, too."

"What brings you in, besides breakfast for the grand-kids?" I asked, trying to keep it friendly and light.

The man's eyes looked troubled, and he cleared his throat. "Our son-in-law unexpectedly passed away here in town." He sighed. "Our daughter and our grandkids are staying with us for a few days."

"Oh, no. I'm very sorry for your loss," I told him, then went to the case to fold up a box and assemble his order.

As I brought the box back to him, his wife connected eyes with me.

"So you're Gracie. I've heard about some of the things you've done. Around River Grove." She spoke in a low voice, her eyes pleading. "Maybe . . ." she started, then looked away. "Do you think we could talk later? That is, if you have some time."

Her husband gave her a look, a quick, barely noticeable shake of the head. Was he discouraging her? He whispered something to his wife—all I heard were the words "public embarrassment."

He could be trying to stop her from airing family trou-bles in public, which honestly, I could see my dad doing. Their generation had a stronger sense of wanting to keep this kind of thing behind closed doors.

"I'm sure you've got your hands full right now," I said sympathetically. "I can talk later for a few minutes, Candace. At 2:30 when we close. Come around to the back door, on the alley."

Her mouth turned up in a grateful smile.

"Thank you, Gracie."

Her husband leaned in toward his wife and frowned as he whispered something. Her husband nodded his thanks to me curtly. They paid for their order then left.

I watched them leave. He had his hand on her back as he shepherded her past the line and through the front door.

What was going on here? The wife seemed like she wanted to talk about her son-in-law's death. Her husband didn't want that to happen.

I wanted to find out why.

I was probably as eager to talk to Candace Muller as she was to talk to me.

Chapter Eleven

Tuesday, *October 21*

Around 8:30 a.m., the chief and the mayor came in and took their place in line, deep into a conversation that didn't look entirely friendly.

When I heard Mayor C's sharp voice say, "Dave, you need to get this wrapped up *soon,*" I knew what they were talking about.

When they came up to the counter, the chief just muttered, "Our usual, Gracie," and pulled out his credit card which he tapped distractedly on the counter while I entered their orders in the POS system.

He wore his usual look when he was in the middle of an investigation: rumpled clothes, bloodshot eyes, uneven grey stubble on his chin. On his breath, I caught the whiff of cheap coffee, which he'd probably gotten at the local gas station or The Corner Market.

My guess was, he hadn't slept much since Saturday night.

I leaned over the counter. "How's it going?"

The chief rolled his eyes and cast the briefest of looks at Mayor C, who was scrolling through messages on her phone.

"I'm meeting with Candace Muller after closing," I said in almost a whisper. "She wants to talk to me."

"Must be nice," the chief said gruffly in a low voice. "I didn't get much from Tom Muller yesterday at their house; he claimed he didn't know anything about his son-in-law's goings-on and didn't think anything he said would be helpful to us."

"Alrighty then," I said brightly, as I handed him a plate with a kale tart for Mayor C and a lone, limp-looking fried egg for him, prepared by Beck in the back room to accommodate his low-carb diet. "If it helps, he didn't want his wife to talk to me either. He hissed something to his wife about her making the family 'a public embarrassment.'"

"You want to stop by city hall later?" He asked hopefully as he and the mayor moved on to the pickup window. I rolled my eyes and gave him a smile as I thought of my day, including the fact that I'd just offered a chunk of my time to Candace Muller.

"I've got all the time in the world."

"Oh, Corinne," I whispered, with a nod in her direction. "Got a minute? I want to talk about Amy Bradshaw. Or Amy Muller, as you probably knew her. It would help with my schedule if we could take a quick walk with Biga."

"Sure." The mayor shrugged listlessly, probably still unhappy with ticket sales. "I'll tell you what I can."

When Maeve came up to relieve me at the front counter, I headed for the back room to check on Biga and get him ready for the walk.

There was a strong aroma of cake in the air—rich, deep

and chocolatey. It was even stronger than the scent of the brioche loaves baking—which considering their irresistible, buttery scent, was hard to beat.

Beck was checking her timer. "Five more minutes and I take it out." She stifled a yawn.

"Make sure you don't fall asleep before then," I joked. She looked back at me sheepishly.

I went into Biga's pen and attached his leash to his harness.

I slipped my down jacket on over my apron and headed out the back steps with my dog. Mayor C met us there, holding her latte.

"Thanks, Gracie. I need to get out and move," the mayor said. "If I stay in my office, I'll keep checking ticket sales."

A bright glimmer of sun seared the edges of the clouds this morning, yet the air was still cool and brisk, making my legs want to move. Mayor C and I headed across the alley to meet up with the trail.

As I sped up my pace, both my dog and the mayor kept up.

"Corinne, Jeremy Bradshaw's wife went to River Grove High." I said as we walked. "Her name was Amy Muller back then."

"The gymnastics star. Not in my circle." The mayor shook her head, pausing to take a sip of her latte. "I saw her around school here and there. She was one of those people who was friendly to everyone. Since there were quite a few people who weren't friendly to me back then, I appreciated that."

"You didn't know her family?" I asked, as Biga made a pitstop at a clump of weeds.

"Only by reputation," the mayor said. "I did know her brother, Michael. He would have been a couple of years younger. He had some problems and his parents took him out of school."

I turned to her quickly. "Do you know anything about what problems he had?"

"Not sure. He had some kind of a breakdown on campus once, and the police came."

"The police?" I asked. "Did he do anything violent?"

She shook her head and her eyes had a distant look, as if she'd taken a deep dip into the past. "I don't think so. Just a loud outburst, apparently. It was during an assembly. This was around the time school shootings became a thing, so it seemed like an overreaction. He ended up going to a private school after that, and I don't think he graduated. I felt sorry for the kid. He always looked kind of pissed off at the world, but I don't think he had a mean bone in his body. High school can be a cruel place when you're different. His sister was talented and gorgeous, everybody's sweetheart. Everybody thought of Michael as her loser brother."

We walked up to the point where we saw the backside of The Riverside, then turned around again. Biga was happy and trying to win Mayor C over, but she looked wary of him and tried to keep her distance.

"I need to get back to the office," she said. "I'm planning a question and answer time in the green space, to address the town's concerns and see what we can do about the maze at this point."

The mayor did many things well and addressing the public in stressful times was one of them.

"Great idea, Corinne. I'd think that would help. You're not thinking of scrapping the haunted maze, are you?"

She frowned, her brow furrowed.

"We may have to. Gordon and I are meeting after the Q and A to talk." She shook her head. "All the work that went into this from so many people in town. We've been planning this all year."

"That's a tough call to make." I said. "I hope it doesn't come to that."

BACK AT THE BAKERY, the lunch staff was gearing up for a crowd. We'd had several online orders, which was often a good indication of how many customers would show up to eat in person.

I took Biga to his pen then washed my hands. Piles of flatbread and loaves of brioche and harvest bread lay on the racks, cooling.

The delicious smell of chocolate cut through it all, as four round cake layers cooled on racks in Beck's corner.

Beck was nowhere to be seen. Maeve had moved over to the industrial mixer. She had headphones on and was singing along loudly, oblivious.

Rose was up front, manning the front counter and the espresso machine. Then I saw Beck, leaning back in my executive office chair, easily the comfiest seat in the house, her eyes closed and an angelic but exhausted look on her face.

I almost threw up my hands in frustration. She must have stayed up later than she'd said.

I let her doze while I sliced bread for the lunch line and piled a tray with pastries for replenishing the front display case. If she didn't get up by the time I was finished, I'd tap her shoulder and wake her up.

Maeve took her headphones off. "Look at her dozing away like that, her cheeks all rosy. I didn't have the nerve to wake her."

After I covered a tray of sliced bread to bring up to the

lunch line, I went over to the chair and leaned toward Beck's ear.

"Beck, it's 10:30," I said softly. "Lunch servers will be here in fifteen minutes."

Her eyes popped open and she sat bolt upright, a look of horror on her face.

"Oh my God, Gracie. I'm so sorry! I couldn't keep my eyes open. I'm awake now." She got up and hurried back to her cake in progress. This was her test cake, which she'd slather with raspberry filling, assemble and frost—then test out the placement of her sculpted decorations. Happily, she told me and the staff we could each take slices home for dessert tonight. The entire staff had been lingering near her station, just waiting for that moment.

Elise and Daisy came in the back door, and soon Beck was wide awake and back in the action, telling them about the bread offerings today.

I'd talk to her this afternoon about her late nights. Her nap hadn't caused any disruptions to our schedule, but I worried about her health. Staying up late then getting up early wasn't a sustainable lifestyle. I'd done that in my first job in the tech industry and went around with bags under my eyes and no energy for two years.

After Maeve closed the front doors for us at 2:30 p.m. that afternoon, I mixed a batch of dough for the harvest grain loaves, then set it in the proofer for its bulk rise, savoring the earthy smell of rye and whole wheat.

I heard a tap at the back door. A small lady in a blue down jacket waved from the window.

I opened the door and led Candace Muller in. Her lined face was pale, and her eyes had the same bloodshot look they'd had this morning. She looked very nervous.

"Let's talk in the dining area," I said with a friendly smile. "Can I get you coffee? Tea?"

"Oh, I'd love a cup of tea," she said with a sigh of relief.

Rose had just finished wiping down tables in the dining area, so I steered Mrs. Muller toward a spot in the back of the room.

I went to get her tea. Always prepared, Rose had heard us talking and was one step ahead of me. She had a cup of hot water on a saucer, with a PG Tips teabag.

I set it down in front of the woman.

"I am so sorry for your loss, Mrs. Muller."

Her hands trembled as she raised the cup to her mouth and blew on it to cool it down.

"I'm afraid it's my grandchildren who are feeling the loss." She set the cup down. "Jeremy wasn't the best of husbands to our Amy, but his children loved him."

"He wasn't a good husband? In what way?" I asked innocently, wondering if she would confirm the rumors.

Candace Muller swallowed. "Our son-in-law had a straying eye." She took a sip of her tea and closed her eyes as if gathering courage to continue. "First there was a fling with his assistant at Arrowfind. Amy found out and confronted him. He swore this had been a mistake and begged her to forgive him. He ended it, and the assistant took a job in the company's east coast office."

I studied her face. "But there were more after that."

"There were rumors, but Amy trusted Jeremy after his apology and wanted to give him the benefit of the doubt. Honestly, our son-in-law could charm the pants off a snake." She shook her head. "Then, finally, last month, we heard about Steve Rawlins's wife, Shayla. Steve had hired a private detective to track his wife and Jeremy. The detective sent back photos of Jeremy and Shayla in a hotel suite in

San Francisco, where he was supposed to be for a technology convention. Also, the detective gave him photocopies of credit card receipts. For flowers and some fancy clothes."

She settled back in her seat and took a sip of tea.

"My husband went ballistic after he heard about this. He called Jeremy and threatened him. Told him he'd make sure he'd never see his kids again."

Candace Muller's words opened a new field of suspects. Besides Steve Rawlins, we now had Tom Muller, who had been furious at his son-in-law. Maybe even Amy Bradshaw herself, when she finally saw proof she couldn't deny.

"This is just . . . a mess." Candace shook her head after a sip of tea. "I don't want my grandchildren to know about this. I'd do anything to keep this from touching them. They're wonderful kids. Sweet and smart."

Their dad was a public figure and news of his murder had been all over the internet.

"Unfortunately, they will find out at some point," I said.

"You're right," the woman said, dabbing her eyes with a napkin. She pressed her lips together tightly. "We should have done something sooner."

I wasn't quite sure what she meant by this. This was their daughter's marriage. What did they think could they *do*?

I did wonder if I should add Candace to my list of suspects. Then the thought came to me.

"Candace, does anyone in your family own a gun?"

She blinked at me, confused, like I was speaking another language.

"Do we have one at the house, you mean?"

I nodded.

"Michael had one. Maybe he still does. He used to hunt

rabbits." As a recent resident of urban Seattle, my first instinct was shock. But I knew guns were a part of life in our rural area.

I was keeping a mental suspect list. Pretty much all the Mullers were on it now.

Candace peered at me pleadingly, her blue eyes big and owl-like, behind her glasses.

"Gracie—would you be able to talk to Amy?"

"Sure, but would she *want* to talk to me? With everything you've told me, she's got a lot on her mind."

Candace Muller thought about this and nodded.

"I'll talk to her and let you know. I think she'd appreciate talking to someone closer to her age. I do believe she wants to know who killed Jeremy."

Unless she killed him herself, I thought cynically.

After I let Candace out the back door, I joined my staff for prep and clean up, as we listened to one of Maeve's playlists of Irish pop.

Beck was quiet as she sliced day-old bread for French toast sticks and loaded the bread "fries" into large ziplock bags for frying tomorrow. Her test cake sat on a plate in her work corner, layered, level, and perfectly frosted. There were marks on the top where she'd tested the placement of the decorations.

I wondered if she'd stayed up the past few nights working on her decorations and hadn't been able to admit it to me.

It was such a strange thing. Beck had the strongest work ethic of anyone I knew. She literally did not *rest* until she'd finished whatever she was working on—or lent a hand to any other staff member who needed help.

But maybe Beck had hit her limit.

I went over to talk to her.

"You okay?"

Her face turned red. "Gracie, I'm so ashamed. I can't believe I fell asleep. In *your* chair." She shook her head. "I don't know how I could have done that."

"How late did you *really* stay up last night?" I asked, watching her face. "Or the night before? It adds up. I know you get really into what you're making and it's hard for you to stop."

She frowned. "Maybe? Time passes when I'm making things. I don't even notice how long I've been working."

"I'm telling you as your boss and as somebody who cares about you," I said, cringing as I heard the lecturing tone in my voice, "you can't stay up really late *and* work baker's hours. I'm speaking from experience. Eventually you'll fall apart. Or fall asleep."

She met my eyes, a sober look on her face. "You're right. I'll try to be more careful, Gracie."

I leaned over her work area and inhaled the aroma from the cake.

"You were serious about sharing this cake with the staff, weren't you?"

Beck grinned, returning to her old self. "Of course. When I'm done prepping these, I'll cut it and wrap pieces for you guys."

"I'm going over to the maze in just a few minutes, Gracie," Rose said, as she came into the back room. "I'm getting excited for opening night on Friday. The actors are so into their parts right now, and they look a-*maze*-ing, if I say so myself."

Over by the industrial mixer, Maeve let out a snort at the bad pun.

Then Rose's phone buzzed. She sobered as she checked a text. "Peony just texted me that Mayor C is thinking of canceling the maze, since ticket sales are down. You don't think that's going to happen, do you, Gracie?" She knew I talked to the mayor about things like this. She studied my face for clues.

Like so many other River Grovians—especially the younger ones—Rose had worked long hours on the maze. This had been a genuine community effort—the largest scale project I'd seen since I'd moved to River Grove. The enthusiasm, especially from the young people and the downtown business volunteers, had been infectious.

I told her what I knew.

"Mayor C's doing a public Q & A at the green space tomorrow at lunch. She wants to fill everyone in on the case and talk about the security measures the chief is putting in place."

I hoped Mayor C would again work her mayoral magic, and the community would be reassured.

Beck had moved over to her cake and was now slicing it into large chunks. She pulled out paper plates and began plating the towering slices, stabilizing them with a spatula and her hand so they didn't fall apart.

Rose, her bag loaded with makeup, eased over to Beck, excited.

"Can I take mine now? This is going to be my dinner over at the maze."

Beck laughed. "Let me wrap it and give you a fork."

She pulled a plastic fork from our lunch supplies, rolled it up in a napkin, and placed it on top of the slice. She wrapped everything up in plastic wrap and handed it to Rose.

"Thanks, Beck!" Rose balanced it in one hand as she headed for the back door.

"Please don't you dare tell Sam I let you have cake for dinner, or he'll ask for it at home."

Rose laughed and pushed open the back door, heading to work on a maze that would hopefully still be able to open on Friday night.

At 4 p.m., I realized I'd forgotten to check in with the chief. I didn't really have time to pop over to city hall to chat.

I saw a text from him.

Time to talk? Let me know.

I responded.

Come over here?

Ten minutes later, he knocked on the front door. I let him in, and we took a seat at the back of the dining area.

The chief was frustrated with the case. I could tell that right away.

I knew why. He wanted very badly to arrest Steve Rawlins. But he couldn't. At least, not yet.

"This may be a motive for Rawlins to murder Jeremy, but right now I need to fill in some blanks, so I can prove Rawlins had the opportunity and the *means* to do it. A few summers ago, I didn't take the time to do that." He shrugged, his face turning red. I remembered his quick arrest of one of The Riverside's sound setup team for the murder of rockstar Noah Bell. The chief had wanted to show the world that our town was vigilant in rooting out crime.

I appreciated the personal growth that made the chief's

confession to me possible. After all, he and the mayor had fought for at least a month about that arrest.

But if Steve Rawlins did kill Jeremy, I wanted the chief to get that evidence and arrest him *soon*. An arrest, especially when it wasn't a local, would help reassure River Grovians that the maze was safe.

"Why is this so hard?" I slumped down in my chair, groaning with frustration. "Jeremy and Steve have a big argument. Steve is furious. A half hour later and really close by, we find Jeremy's body in the maze."

"If you're so smart, put the pieces together, Gracie." The chief looked at me soberly. "The pieces we have just don't fit. Yes, Jeremy Bradshaw was shot in the maze. But I heard back from the coroner. It turns out he wasn't shot with the handgun Rawlins had with him. He came in to drop that off this morning. I could tell it was the wrong gun right away. The bullet that killed Bradshaw was rifle ammunition. A long thin bullet."

"Well, that's unfortunate," I said, feeling our hopes for an arrest fade fast.

The chief continued.

"Also, no one spotted Rawlins going into the maze and leaving. And there were still a few people there working on the maze. Nobody saw anything or any person who wasn't supposed to be there."

I slumped back in my chair.

"Well, when you put it that way . . . " I frowned.

He was right. As my father would tell me, you couldn't draw a conclusion from just two data points. It wasn't that simple.

"We're also waiting to hear the results of DNA testing in the area of the maze. The crime scene team scoured the place that morning after. It takes a while to get results from the lab. If we're lucky, we'll hear within a week or two."

While waiting for test results, did it make any sense for me to look into this murder? Maybe the truth would be determined by tests. *Science.*

Information I couldn't get from talking to people around town.

Suddenly, I felt deflated.

The case had already wedged itself into my mind, and I didn't want to give up thinking about it.

"Every case is different," the chief said. "You're decent at detective work, Gracie, and you have good insight into people. But this one may be decided by forensic evidence, not your intuition."

Maybe it would. But there were still leads I wanted to follow up on.

And I planned on doing that.

Chapter Twelve

Tuesday evening, October 21

Total step count for Tuesday: 7,259

After closing up the bakery, I drove home to drop off Biga with my father and Mary Jo, so Elana and I could have our night out.

Mary Jo had been trying hard to cultivate a good relationship with my dog. Her efforts were paying off—sort of. When Mary Jo gave him a table scrap, he was 100 percent on Team Mary Jo, ready to cuddle.

But when she and my dad were watching a movie, and Mary Jo really wanted Biga to come up and sit on her lap, he couldn't be bothered. He was off to lick food residue off the kitchen floor.

Elana came by to pick me up at 6:30 p.m. She'd come from work, so she was dressed better for going out to eat than I was, wearing sassy little ankle boots, cigarette slacks, and a tailored, cropped jacket. I was still dusting flour off my jeans, though I'd managed to pick out a fancier top in just the right shade of red that looked good on me.

"Are you up for some place in Santa Cruz?" Elana asked as I opened the passenger side door. "I'm craving, maybe, Thai or Indian? I need me some *spice.*"

"Sounds good to me. I'm just hungry," I said, distractedly. I was still mulling over what Candace Muller had told me today about Steve's wife and Jeremy Bradshaw.

"Indian it is. There's a nice place on Mission Street in Santa Cruz. I'm craving butter chicken."

"Curry sounds good to me," I said with a smile. Maybe Elana was right; I needed to get out of my River Grove/Laughing Loaf bubble and enjoy something.

"Nate comes back when?"

"Monday night. I was hoping the case would keep my mind busy and I'd get it figured out by the time he got back. That would have been nice—then we could debrief when he got back. I mean, since he and I were the ones who found the body and all. I could give him a play-by-play of what he missed."

I suddenly wondered if that would be my version of my dad and Reggie's detailed and tedious replays of the moves in one of their chess games.

"Yeah, but *gurrrl*—" Elana steered us toward the main highway, through River Grove downtown, most of it dimmed as businesses had shut down for the day. "Nate's been gone this week, and you haven't had any fun at all. You've been working from before dawn at the bakery till sunset. Which of course is your *job.* Then brainstorming about the case, doing some research, and taking care of your needy little dog. It's time to kick out the jams, baby!"

I snorted, amused. "Did you time travel here from the 1970s? Fine then. Let's do something crazy."

Elana and I weren't always on the same page as far as having fun.

"Here's my theory," she frowned as she guided the car down the redwood-lined highway in the direction of the coast. "You need to do something totally different. It will rearrange your thoughts, Gracie. Activate your subconscious, and your thinking will change. You'll have a breakthrough in the case in no time."

A gross simplification, maybe, but there was something to what Elana said. I was in a comfortable rut of work and home. Not that either were bad, but a change could be a good thing.

After finding parking on the street, Elana and I joined the line at the restaurant. In front of us were two twentysomethings on a date, an older couple with an aging hippie vibe, and several twentysomething men who looked like they worked in tech. Some of them were discussing a software coding change they'd dealt with that day at work, with the intense excitement of relating the plot of a new blockbuster movie they'd seen.

Elana was in a very good mood tonight. She'd recently transferred to a new department, and she was getting along well with her new boss.

"I don't dread going to work anymore." She applied a quick swipe of gloss to her lips. "I just found out that Todd, my predecessor in the old job, was laid off last week. I feel sorry for the guy, but I also feel vindicated. I got tired of being blamed for things he didn't do." She pored over a menu with a satisfied smile. "I know the tech industry can be fickle," she said as she considered the spice levels on the butter chicken. "And who knows, I could be replaced by AI any day. But it feels good to start off with a boss who supports and appreciates me."

Elana had gone through a year of stress in a new job she'd dreamed of, only to find out she was replacing an employee who had friends in high places and absolutely no work ethic at all.

"It's about time, Elana."

We heard a voice pipe up from somewhere in the line behind us.

One of the tech bros behind us called out to Elana. "Hey, don't you work at Forte Systems? I've seen you in the cafeteria."

She turned around. "My name's Elana Schiffer," she said with a smile. "I'm in product marketing now. You guys in engineering?" The group nodded, Adam's apples on their thin necks bobbing in alignment.

"We're programmers," one of the guys called out. "Most of us are still at Forte. But Chien and Aveer here work across the street at Arrowfind. We have lunch with them all the time."

My ears perked up. Steve Rawlins' company. It was a fairly big one. These engineering guys probably wouldn't be on a first name basis with their company's legal counsel. Would they even know him?

"Why don't you guys join us?" Elana said expansively. "This is my friend Gracie. She used to work in tech, but she runs a bakery now. When she's not investigating crime in her small town, that is."

The group of young men looked at us excitedly. "Yeah, sure. Let's get a bigger table."

One of the guys looked in the door at the waiter who was taking names for the wait list. He pushed his way through the couples in line to let the waiter know.

I was tired, and not sure I wanted to spend an hour or two making conversation with a group of techies. But maybe Elana had been right. Taking on a new experience could be a good thing.

And there was that Arrowfind connection.

After ten minutes of lively conversation about video games and one of the guy's recent gambling spree in Las Vegas, I decided to ask about Steve Rawlins.

"I heard Arrowfind's legal counsel got into some trouble over in River Grove," I said to Aveer and Chien.

Chien gave me a look of complete puzzlement. But Aveer turned toward me and lowered his voice. He was probably seven or eight years younger than me, a nice-looking man with soulful dark eyes.

"I've heard some people talking about him," he said. "He disappeared a few days ago. Nobody's saying where he is, but his assistant tells everyone he's on a business trip setting up a merger. I've heard he's a murder suspect. 'The River Grove Maze Murder,' they're calling it."

Sounds like Aveer had read all the local news stories.

Unfortunately for Mayor C and her maze publicity efforts, Maze Murder made for a really catchy headline.

The waiter brought out our dishes, which smelled fragrant with spices.

"What's Steve Rawlins like?" I asked Aveer, after I'd heaped lemongrass curry and basmati rice onto my plate. Aveer filled his plate with naan and pieces of bright orange tandoori chicken, cooked in the restaurant's clay oven.

He shrugged.

"Nice guy. Very friendly. Brings his kids in sometimes. From what I've heard, he's a great dad."

"Did Jeremy Bradshaw visit Arrowfind very often? I heard the two of them were good friends."

A shadow seemed to cross the young man's face. He suddenly changed. Now he chose his words carefully.

"Bradshaw used to work there. He did a few talks on AI at Arrowfind. He was working on a project with Steve." He took a gulp of his Singha beer. "When I heard Rawlins was a person of interest in Bradshaw's death, I was shocked. He couldn't have done it."

"So you met Bradshaw?" I asked.

Aveer thought for a while then nodded, almost reluctantly.

"What did you think of him?" I asked with an encouraging smile.

Aveer downed a quick gulp of beer like he needed it. "He's been talking about making AI honest. And setting reasonable limits on it. I think it's all BS." There was anger in his tone.

I snorted. "I'm thinking the same thing. Wouldn't that be nice. But when I saw an ad for Generistic's product a few days ago, it didn't mention honest or ethical AI."

Aveer went on to give his opinions about AI. Some of it was interesting, but most of it was beyond my understanding.

After a while, a goofy smile came over his face, and he started asking more about me personally.

After telling him about the bakery and a bit about my tech past, I connected eyes with Elana, who was across the table, listening to a conversation about a gaming convention and looking utterly bored. She widened her eyes in desperation and gave me a *get me out of here now* look.

"Thanks for the conversation, Aveer. My friend and I have another meetup soon, so I need to leave." I laid out cash to cover my meal and portion of the tip.

"I very much hope we meet again," Aveer said with a

wistful smile, his dark brown eyes gleaming in the candle-light. He took a card out of his pocket.

AVEER GULATI
Software Engineer
Arrowfind
408-555-8818 ext 477
Bayview Technical Park
Sunnyvale, California

Outside, Elana and I took deep breaths of the cool, damp ocean air, feeling the exhilaration of our quick escape.

"I never want to hear about role-playing games again," Elana said with a groan. "I was wedged right in the middle of that group. It was like being held hostage."

I giggled, then soon I was laughing and couldn't stop myself. Maybe it was letting loose with the stresses of the case.

"Gracie, this is *serious*," my friend said insistently as we walked toward her car. "I don't want to hear about trolls, or dungeons and dragons, or dice throws or spells. That was an hour of my life that I will never get back."

"You were right about having a completely new experience to make me think about the case differently," I said, sobering up, as we spotted our car in the distance. The muffled sounds of an electric guitar and drums spilled out of a local restaurant, live music trailing out into the night. A damp, salty ocean smell drifted in on a breeze from the bay.

"Aveer knows both Steve Rawlins and Jeremy Bradshaw," I said as we got into the car. "He told me some things about Steve Rawlins. But there was something about how he said it," I said, remembering his nervous looks as I asked him about Bradshaw. "I think he knows more than what he told me."

"Think you can get it out of him without leading him on?" Elana looked over at me as she started the car. "Girl, I saw the way he looked at you."

Four more days until Nate's return.

I sighed heavily.

"Yeah, there's that."

That night, Nate called at 9 p.m., and we continued talking past our usual time. He listened to my progress on the case and asked about everyone at the bakery.

He texted me pictures he'd taken, and a few videos of crazy animal behavior he'd observed. In one video, a crow dropped nuts from a branch high up in a tree. When they cracked far below, the crow would swoop down to pick at the shells and eat their contents.

"I always thought of crows as the lowlifes of the bird world," I said, in awe. "Now I have a new respect for them."

"I'm looking forward to seeing you again," he said, his voice low, rumbly, and sexy as hell, as if talking about crow behavior was some kind of aphrodisiac. "Can I come over when I get into town?"

"My dad'll be with Mary Jo when you get back, but I'll be here. Can't wait to see you."

I said this even though, deep inside, I was still grumbling about his suggestion that I should "get outside more often and walk." I missed him, but I planned to follow up on that comment.

After we hung up, I went to the hall to look at myself in the full-length mirror again. Seriously? What could he have been talking about?

I looked at my step counter. I'd started transferring my daily steps to a spreadsheet in a show of full-on nerd behavior. If I could make fun of my boyfriend saying he was a bird nerd, he could easily make fun of me for being a data nerd. I was constantly tweaking and updating my spreadsheet for bakery sales and tracking the cost of those sales.

Now I opened the steps spreadsheet on my computer and saw my step total getting higher every day. My goal was to have a total of 70,000 steps for the time he was up in Oregon. I'd done this because I wanted to prove something.

I might have taken it the wrong way, but he'd implied that I was spending my day sitting around the bakery, nibbling on scones and tarts. In fact, almost half of my steps were from my time at the bakery. I was constantly moving during my workday.

I was tired tonight.

I changed for bed and peeled back the comforter to burrow in for the night. Biga, sensing it was bedtime, trotted into my room and jumped up on the bed.

"Goodnight, Biga boy. Thinking positive thoughts right now," I said to him because, of course, he would understand.

"We're going to figure out this case soon. And at the end of the week, your second favorite person will come home from Oregon and give you all the cuddles you want."

Chapter Thirteen

WEDNESDAY, *October 22*

THE NEXT DAY, as the bakery hit its midmorning lull, I decided to wrap up a box of treats to take over to Candace Muller and her family.

I had an ulterior motive, big time. If I was going to take this case seriously, I needed to meet the family, including Amy, and if I was lucky, this younger brother Michael, who "scared people."

I assembled a pink bakery box and filled it with tarts and cinnamon rolls, then set it into a Laughing Loaf carrier bag.

I texted, asking if it would be okay for me and my little dog to come over to drop off some goodies. By this time, Candace should have talked to her daughter and Amy would be willing to talk to me.

Candace got back to me pretty quickly.

Please!

The kids would love to see your dog. They
need a distraction.

I'D TAKE the river trail to the Mullers', heading in the
opposite direction of The Riverside.

This would be a longer walk than I usually did, but, hey,
think of all the steps I'd rack up. And I did. It would be my
first 10,000 step day.

The Muller's house was a large, two-story house set
back a hundred feet from the river, with a tidy, well land-
scaped front yard, not typical of that area of River Grove,
where abandoned cars and weeds were the norm. Redwood
trees provided a canopy of shade for the house.

I rang the doorbell, and instead of Candace, a boy about
seven or eight answered the door.

"Hello. You have a dog?" he asked, his eyes lighting up
when he saw Biga.

Candace appeared at the door, her eyes still red-
rimmed. She held her grandson to her.

"Gracie, come on in," she opened the door wide and
waved us in. "This is Charlie, my grandson."

Charlie couldn't take his eyes off Biga. "Can I play with
him? What's his name?"

"Biga," I said. "He's named for a kind of bread I make.
He's friendly, but you need to put your hand out and let
him smell you first. He'll try to get at any food you have, so
make sure you don't leave anything out where he can get it.
He's obsessed with food."

Charlie laughed and got down on his knees and put his

hand out to Biga, who sniffed it then looked around for what he was really interested in—crumbs of anything dropped on the floor.

"Gracie from the bakery brought us some pastries," Candace said, as we walked into the living room. An older girl, maybe twelve, was curled up on the couch under a crocheted afghan, reading a book.

"This is Luna here, reading. The kids will be with us for at least this week."

"Charlie, have you ever had a pet dog?" I asked the boy.

He shook his head, continuing to stare at the dog with fascination.

I dug inside my handbag for Biga's bag of treats.

"You can feed him a treat if you like." I went over and dropped two treats in the boy's hand.

Luna looked up from her book a few times. Finally, she set it aside and started watching.

Charlie tried to get Biga to jump for a treat, and a minute later, Luna slid down onto the floor to play with the dog.

Biga liked how this was going for him. He'd been relegated to his pen all morning. He was now the star of the show.

A blonde woman wandered absent mindedly into the room. She stood near the doorway to the kitchen, scrolling through her phone. This must be Amy Bradshaw. She was petite and athletic, shorter even than I was, and had blonde curly hair. She was in her early forties, but she didn't look much older than me.

Was she a grieving widow? I couldn't tell yet. She wore sweatpants and a faded blue UCLA t-shirt. No makeup, and the fact that her blue eyes were bloodshot made them look almost violet.

Amy Bradshaw finally noticed me. She gave me an offhand look, as if I were a door-to-door salesperson or takeout food deliverer.

Candace cleared her throat.

"Amy, this is Gracie Markley, from the bakery. The one who's solved a few—" she seemed about to say *murders*, then looked down at the children on the floor. "--uh, *cases* around River Grove."

Amy sighed heavily. I recognized the look on her face. It wasn't full-on grief. It wasn't sorrow. It was something I'd felt before: betrayal. Between the photos the PI took in San Francisco and the father of her children being murdered, maybe she still didn't know how she felt.

"Hi, Gracie," she said sullenly and then shot a look at her mother and frowned. "Really, mom? Why did you do this?"

"I thought Gracie could help, dear," Candace said, flustered, looking like she'd regretted ever talking to me about her son-in-law's murder.

"You could have asked me. This is *my* life, not yours." Amy kept her voice at a low tone, but it was shaking. "I'm 43, not twelve."

Candace cast a cautious look at Luna and Charlie on the floor with Biga. But with the dog as entertainment, the kids were oblivious to their conversation.

"I only wanted to help," the woman said nervously.

This felt awkward. Candace hadn't even talked to her daughter about me. Well-meaning or not, Candace had blindsided her daughter, and I felt bad for her. I tried to think of an escape plan.

"You don't have to talk to me, Amy," I said, with a sympathetic nod. "I can't imagine what you must be feeling right now."

Amy sized me up, then heaved a sigh and raised a hand toward the hallway.

"Let's talk in my old bedroom," she said, heading around the corner. "It's a gymnastics hall of fame, just warning you."

I left Biga with Candace and the kids. He was in the living room, searching the rug for crumbs like I was sniffing for clues.

Family photos lined the hall as we walked down it. There were photos of Amy as a teenager, one on uneven bars and one where she was caught, mid-handspring, during a floor exercise at a gymnastics competition. A gold-framed certificate on the wall said, "AMY BRADSHAW, GYMNASTICS COACH OF THE YEAR."

Then, there was the whole family in front of a camper in Yosemite, with Amy and Michael as young children. There were a couple of graduation photos of Amy from River Grove High School. Then in front of the Muller house, a photo of a teenaged boy who was not smiling. His eyes bored into the camera, his mouth pressed closed as if to keep inside something that he wanted to let out.

Then it hit me. This was a younger version of the man I'd seen at Corner Market.

Amy opened the door to a room with a white four-poster bed and a purple futon-like loveseat. Gold trophies, from small to enormous, lined a bookshelf that ran across two walls of the room.

"Have a seat." Amy motioned to the futon as she lay back against the pillows on her bed. "What do you want to know? What would be helpful? I've heard some of the things you've done, Gracie. Don't think I'm dissing you. My mom put me in a tough spot. Like she has to fix my problems for me. I've dealt with this all my life. It gets old after a while."

"You're a grown-up with two kids. You run your own coaching business." I looked over at her trophies. "And you've obviously done very well at gymnastics tournaments."

"How did you know?" Amy rolled her eyes and let out a frustrated laugh.

"Your mom came to the bakery to talk to me. My boyfriend Nate and I were the ones who found Jeremy in the maze that night."

Amy swallowed hard and frowned. "I didn't know that. I'm sorry."

"I found out you were from River Grove Monday night. But I'm curious. Why would Jeremy be having dinner with Steve in River Grove that night at The Riverside? Did he have connections in River Grove other than your family?"

She shook her head. "I know they were working together on something for Generistic. Jeremy and Steve had been friends since they worked together at Arrowfind. Our families went on vacations together—which is painful to think about, after the detective's report." Her lips twisted and she looked down.

"Different issue than yours," I said, "but I understand some of what you might be feeling. Four years ago, I found out my husband was living a double life."

The muscles in Amy's face visibly relaxed. "I should have known," she said. "I shouldn't have trusted him again."

I nodded. I didn't need to jump in with more of my experience.

"It sounds like you want to find out who killed Jeremy."

"I do. For my kids. They adored their dad. The weird thing is that a person can completely fail in one area of life and at the same time be pretty good in another. He was a good dad. A fun dad. They're going to miss him." She swiped at her eyes with the back of her hand. "They should know who took him away from them."

"Jeremy and Steve were arguing in The Riverside that night," I said. "Steve accused Jeremy of a few things. He said Jeremy had cheated him out of something—maybe some kind of business deal gone bad. Later I found out about Steve's wife."

"Shayla," Amy said, with no bitterness in her tone. I left space for her to continue, maybe to rant about the woman, but she didn't.

"That makes Steve the number one suspect right now," I said. "Unfortunately, he's left town."

"There's no way Steve would kill anybody," Amy said calmly. "He doesn't have it in him. He's not wired that way."

"Maybe so, but he's got two big things going against him. His public argument with Jeremy and the fact that Jeremy was found in the maze outside The Riverside that night, after they met."

Amy shook her head firmly. "I've known him and Shayla for twelve years. It's not possible."

I thought of the crimes I'd seen happen in River Grove. "Sometimes people do things you think they'd never do in a million years."

She closed her eyes and lay her head back on her pillow. "I choose to believe that there are people out there who are better than that."

"There are. I've met one," I said, thinking of Nate up in the Oregon wilderness.

I was still hearing gleeful laughter and the scampering

of my dog from down the hall. Biga was a happy diversion for these kids today.

"Amy, I need to know a few things from you, if you do want me to help," I said, when Amy opened her eyes again.

"Okay," she said cautiously, as she sat up on the bed.

"If not Steve, could there be someone else who had a grudge against Jeremy? Maybe someone who thinks Jeremy cheated them in a business deal. Or maybe another spouse of a woman he was seeing."

"I wouldn't have a clue about that last one," Amy said with an expression of disgust. "But Jeremy did disrupt the industry when he launched his company. He took what he needed as far as expertise and even staff from other companies. Pretty brazenly. I'm sure he made a lot of people mad. But then I'm not the best person to ask on that point either. I'm not in tech."

"He didn't receive any threats that you know of?" I asked, watching her face.

Amy laughed drily. "I'm sure he did."

"Okay, just asking this, Amy, since I don't know. Did your brother Michael know about the things Jeremy was doing? About Shayla?"

She sighed. "He might have overheard something. Sometimes I think he knows more than he says." Then she sat up on the bed. "You're not suggesting that Michael had anything to do with Jeremy's murder?"

"I don't know. I'm just asking," I said. I'd heard indignation building in her voice.

"He would never do anything like that. Not Michael."

It was probably not a good idea to press it further. But I did.

"Not even if it was on your behalf? To protect you?"

A sudden look came over Amy's face—the look of a

drawbridge being pulled up. "Our conversation is over, Gracie. I'm not going to talk about this anymore."

I wouldn't get anything else from her, and I could understand. She was wading through her own feelings, dealing with unhelpful parents, and trying to be there for her children as they coped with loss.

"Thank you for talking to me, Amy. If you can think of anything else—anyone who could have done this, let me know."

I walked back down the hall to the living room. I looked up, suddenly face-to-face with Michael, who shouldered past me on his way to a door at the end of the hall. Before the door slammed, his face twisted into a scowl.

Then the entire mood changed when I took eight more steps and entered a living room filled with utter joy.

Charlie was playing with Biga, trying to get him to chase a plastic toy.

"Biga, run for it!" he said as he threw the toy down the hall. Biga dutifully scampered down the hall after it.

Luna tucked her hair behind her ears and sat down cross-legged on the floor watching the dog as he trotted back with the toy. She tried to get him to come to her.

"He's so cute!" She stared at Biga with a look of awe. "What kind of dog is he, Gracie?"

I took a seat on the floor near Luna.

"He's a Chihuahua Basenji mix. The chihuahua side makes him small and also kind of nervous. The Basenji side gives him a weird, yelpy bark."

"I'm going to ask my mom if we can have a dog," she said resolutely. "It would be so much fun."

"It's a lot of work," I said, trying to be a voice of reason. "You'd have to feed him, keep his water bowl clean, take him outside to do his business and walk him every day. Oh, and give him a bath. Dogs get stinky."

Candace Muller was listening intently as I talked to the kids. "Luna, your mother has a lot of things on her mind right now. So if this is something that you really want, you'd have to do some research about how to care for a dog." The kids looked at each other excitedly as if they were forming a pact—the *Get-a-Dog* pact. "You'll need to learn how to take care of a dog and split up the chores, so your mom isn't doing the work. You and Charlie would have to be very responsible."

Luna and Charlie passed excited looks between them.

"We can do this," Luna said soberly. "And we are willing to do the work."

Charlie gazed affectionately at Biga, who was looking at him with eagerness, tongue hanging out as he panted, waiting for the toy to be thrown.

"Yeah, Charlie, we could read books about it. So we know what the dog needs and eats. We could train him, too," Luna said, a pleading note in her voice.

These kids really wanted a dog. They might be a little too ambitious, but maybe they just needed to find the right breed. Biga hadn't responded super well to the whole training thing.

I stood up.

"I'm sorry to take Biga from you so soon, but we've got to get back to the bakery. Maybe Biga can come visit another time."

The kids groaned at the thought of their new friend leaving but seemed happy at the thought of another chance to see Biga.

Candace Muller saw us to the door. Her demeanor had lightened in the past half hour.

"I can't thank you enough, Gracie. For everything. A dog may be in our future." She gave me a brief hug. "I'll stay in touch."

Biga looked longingly back at the kids standing in the doorway as we walked across the yard. They watched him like a celebrity. My little dog was going to miss this. He wouldn't get this much attention back at the bakery.

I clipped Biga's leash onto his harness and headed for the trail, giving one last glance back at the house.

Before the curtains closed over the far window, I caught a glimpse of curly dark hair.

Someone wanted to make sure we left.

Chapter Fourteen

Wednesday, *October 22*

Total step count for Wednesday: 14,205

By the time I left the Muller's, it was approaching noon.

If I continued on the river trail heading toward downtown, I could still catch Mayor C's Q&A at The Riverside's green space.

It was a mile and a half from the Muller's, but I'd rack up lots of steps. And Biga, after the hike and his playdate with Charlie and Luna Bradshaw, would probably be happy to nap for the rest of the afternoon. A win for everyone.

So far, I'd enjoyed my three days of walking everywhere. I was outdoors in my favorite time of year.

River Grove was a town of walkers and hikers, so I'd met friendly faces everywhere I went. If I could just get rid of the idea that Nate thought I was in serious need of exercise, I could see it as something I'd want to continue.

I still felt like I was trying to prove something to him.

My talk with Amy Bradshaw hadn't shed any light on who murdered Jeremy. She'd said Steve Rawlins, who had the strongest motive, couldn't have possibly killed her husband. But if he hadn't, why was he in hiding?

The chief was probably waiting for the test result, DNA or fingerprints, that would justify him putting a warrant out for the man's arrest.

And Amy refused to think about the possibility of Michael's involvement in the murder. Though, as I thought about it, I could understand. Considering her own brother a murderer was too much with everything else she was dealing with now.

Soon I saw the buildings of downtown. Biga with his pitstops was making this a slow process, but a few pee breaks later, I saw the roof of The Riverside, sheltered by redwoods.

Biga and I made our way to the edge of the green space, where a crowd of about fifty people had gathered, some sitting on the green space benches, and a few sitting on folding camp chairs they'd brought themselves.

Somebody, probably from Reggie's staff, had also set out fancy, padded folding chairs. People were still arriving, walking up from the street. It was a mix of older residents, along with downtown merchants, young adults with toddlers, and a few parents of teens I recognized.

Mayor C, in her bright yellow down jacket and A SMALL TOWN WITH BIG TREES t-shirt, was already addressing the group. She stood right in front of the haunted maze, with spider legs, moss, and a few bats dangling over the wall behind her. It didn't look nearly as scary as it had in the dark.

"Welcome, everyone. Thank you for coming out today."

She glanced over the group.

"I want to ask you. How many of you have lived in River Grove for at least twenty years?"

About twenty people raised their hands. I recognized Reggie and the Key Haus brothers, Hans and Victor. Then I spotted Annie and Eric Morton, Jeanne Daniels from Speed Spot Motors, Lorrie Delgado from The Corner Market, and Janet from Clip n' Curl along with her husband. Then the parents of teens: the Robbins family, including Skyler; Dakota Li's parents; and Amelia Gruber's parents, Martin and Lisa. Deputy Brad Castro, who I knew was born and raised in River Grove, raised his hand.

"Now how many of you have lived in River Grove for ten years?"

More hands went up. The Chief and his daughter Renee, standing in the back, raised their hands, along with about ten other attendees. Standing next to the chief and his daughter was a man in his thirties wearing a uniform

When the mayor asked for people who'd lived here five years or less, about twenty people raised their hands. These seemed to be people with young children in tow. One of them, a curly headed girl, tried to make a beeline for the maze opening and Mayor C's clown. Her father quickly picked her up and lugged her back.

The major nodded. "Thank you, everyone. Those of you longtime River Grovians know. This is a special town. It's also a town that has its challenges. We've had torrential rainstorms, landslides, wildfires, and, unfortunately, murder."

At that, a loud male voice yelled out from the crowd.

"Don't you get it, Corinne? That's why we're here. It's the *murders*. A community project like the maze is great, but who's going to keep us safe?"

Mayor C looked out at him, unflapped. "Dan, I have an answer to that. We will open up to questions and comments soon."

I took a seat in an empty chair and pulled Biga up on my lap. Within a few minutes, his eyes were closed and he was dozing.

The mayor continued.

"Over the past five years, our population has grown. It's like some of you here: young families who want to escape Silicon Valley or Bay Area traffic. High tech workers who enjoy working remotely in a relaxed, beautiful place. In the past five years, our population has grown by 782."

A wisecracker from the audience, someone I didn't recognize, shot back.

"Yeah, but it was 800 people before the murders started!" Scattered laughter broke out among the group.

The mayor went on to talk about the programs she, Chief Westerman, and the chamber of commerce had put in place to provide increased safety and amenities in town: traffic safety, town events, and improvements to our town baseball "stadium" where the River Rats played.

The mayor was right: even in the short time I'd been in town, there always seemed to be an upcoming town gathering or some improvement being introduced. The mayor and town leadership seemed to be doing a good job.

"And now, I'd like to bring up three people to address the concerns about the maze directly. Welcome Chief Dave Westerman and RGPD Deputy Brad Castro. And our special guest today, County Deputy Sheriff Lyle Scoggins."

The crowd clapped with more enthusiasm than usual. And with the mention of the county sheriff, the crowd began talking among themselves.

I wasn't the only one who knew of the chief's resistance

to asking help from the county. His attitude was that help from the county was neither needed nor wanted.

But it wasn't just the chief himself. When River Grove was first founded in the late 1800s, a provision in the town charter decreed that a town police department be set up, and the town would be policed by their own town force, not the county sheriff's department. The town had held on to this mindset for over a hundred years. So I was very interested in what was happening right now.

The three law enforcement officers came up front and stood while the mayor continued.

"For the maze's two-week run, we will have a constant security presence at the maze." She looked out at the attendees, holding them in a firm, chin-up gaze, the kind that photographers like to capture for new stories.

"Security will be provided by both River Grove PD and the county sheriff's department. We're confident that this strong presence will maintain the maze as a safe activity for our community."

More applause from the people seated at the Q&A. Then the mayor bravely opened up the gathering to questions from the attendees.

"Is it true that the murder took place in the maze itself?"

"The chief and coroner confirmed that Bradshaw was murdered and found in the maze," Mayor C said curtly. "Next question?"

"Can you tell us the status of the investigation into Jeremy Bradshaw's death?"

The mayor acknowledged the question with a nod.

"For that, I will hand the microphone over to Chief Westerman."

The chief took the mic, though he didn't look excited about answering.

"Thank you, Corinne. Right now, we have a chief suspect, a colleague of Bradshaw's. We are waiting on test results we hope will provide confirmation." He nodded curtly and prepared to hand the mic right back to the mayor.

A white-haired woman in a River Rats ball cap stood up and asked her question very loudly. "Why haven't you arrested this person?"

I thought about what the poor, beleaguered chief could say in answer to this.

He shifted on his feet. "We expect an arrest to be forthcoming."

"When?" Someone else asked.

"Yeah, what's the holdup?" Another voice piped up.

"We'd all sleep easier if we knew he was behind bars," said a younger man holding a squirmy toddler.

"I heard the guy skipped town," Jeanne Daniels said, concern in her voice. "Is this true?"

The chief gave a brief bob of the head. "I can't comment any further on our investigation at this time. But when we've arrested him, we will notify the community immediately."

The mayor gave the chief what I'd call a disappointed look. She looked like she considered handing the mic to the sheriff's representative but then thought better of it.

"Thank you for attending today. With the unified support of RGPD and our county sheriff, the maze will open on schedule this Friday." And because she couldn't help herself, she continued. "For tickets, be sure to go to *townofrivergrove.gov*. We're offering a special family discount."

I stood up with Biga, who abruptly woke up, disoriented. The chief was still standing in front of the maze, talking with Deputy Scoggins.

I walked in their direction. Seeing me, the chief wrapped up his conversation with Scoggins with a nod and a nervous laugh and came over to us.

"What made you accept support from the county?" I asked quietly.

"You think that was *my* choice? Corinne gave me an ultimatum," he whispered fiercely, rubbing the back of his neck. "She wanted her damn ticket sales. I hadn't made much progress, so I couldn't turn it down."

I set Biga down, ready to head back to the bakery.

"I just walked over from the Mullers'," I told him in a low voice. "I'm worried about Michael. Candace said in passing that she thinks he has a gun. He used it for hunting rabbits."

The Chief groaned. "Brad and I are on it. Thanks for the heads-up."

Chapter Fifteen

Thursday, *October 23*

Total step count for Thursday: 10,478

We'd been open for an hour, and I was watching our usual morning transition: the noisy exit of the teens, followed by the slow, much quieter influx of adults.

There were the downtown regulars, including the mayor and the chief, and the usual remote workers with laptops. There was also a group of knitters who'd started coming in on Thursdays recently. They ranged in age from early twenties to probably eighties. They ordered their tea and lattes and went to sit down at the big table, where they started taking projects out of their bags and talking quietly amongst themselves.

Then I saw a face I recognized from somewhere else entirely, and it didn't make sense to me to see him here, standing in line waiting to order. It was like when you associate someone with a specific place and time and your brain refuses to accept this person as valid in a different area of your life.

He came up to the counter with a somewhat shy smile.

"Aveer!" I said, wondering why he was here. I also forgot whether I'd told him clearly that I was dating someone.

"Gracie, good to see you again. I was on my way in to work and had to get gas, so I decided to pull off in River Grove."

"Good to see you. What can I get you?"

"A mocha with almond milk and one of those tarts." He pointed to the case, then connected with my eyes. "I also wanted to chat—"

I was beginning to feel uneasy. I wasn't really sure of his motives. He was still giving me those subtle, flirtatious glances from Tuesday night.

"I can't talk now," I said, looking past him at the line. "This is our busiest time of day."

He lowered his voice. "When we were standing in line at the restaurant, your friend, Elana, said you investigated murders, and later it made sense to me. You were asking a lot of questions about Bradshaw and about Steve Rawlins." His expression turned serious. "I need to tell you. I know more than I told you the other night."

I studied his face, including those big, soulful eyes. He seemed to be serious.

"I won't have free time till I take my dog for a walk at 10," I said, as I watched the people in line behind Aveer give me judgy looks. "If you can, meet me at the back steps of the bakery at 10:05 a.m. Right on the alley behind this street."

Aveer looked down at the high-tech watch on his wrist

as if consulting an oracle. He tapped it and looked at something on it, scrolled through a list with his finger, then thought for a moment. He nodded.

"I will see you in the alley at 10:05, Gracie."

What had I just agreed to?

If Aveer could tell me more about Steve Rawlins, it would be worth it. Maybe he knew where the Arrowfind legal counsel had disappeared to.

One thing was becoming clear: all these walks would help me meet my step count goals this month. That was something to report back to Nate on.

As the morning got busier, I didn't even think about my meetup with Aveer. While Beck took over the espresso machine, Rose was busy filling sheet pans with flatbread, which we'd need a lot of in a couple of hours. Rose was a quick learner, but she'd needed basic instructions, and Maeve was too busy with the brioche and sourdough to go through them with her.

As it approached 10 a.m., the bread situation was under control, and all items were ready for the lunch service. I told Maeve and Rose I needed to take the dog out and would be back within twenty minutes.

I put on Biga's collar and leash and scooped him up to go out the back door. I opened the door to see Aveer standing at the bottom of the steps.

Biga looked up at the young man, the beginnings of a growl in his throat, unsure if he was to be trusted.

"Hi, Gracie," he nodded, then continued in a serious tone. "So this is your little dog. What exactly is his job at the bakery?"

I laughed at this attempt to ease the tension. "Biga's in charge of eating up anything we drop on the floor. Let's head down the river trail. Have you seen much of River Grove?"

"Only its gas stations," he said sheepishly. "And The Riverside Saloon, where I've had some meetings."

We walked across the alley and toward the trail, where a couple of very focused joggers passed us. Once they were a hundred yards ahead of us, Aveer looked around us to make sure we were alone, then began talking.

"A year and a half ago, Bradshaw approached Steve Rawlins about launching his company. He'd prepared a business plan, and it looked great on paper. Since I have experience with AI, Steve brought me in, too. Steve vouched for Jeremy, since the two had been friends for years. So Steve and I invested in Generistic, and we helped him get other backers."

"You both invested in the company," I repeated. "How much, if you don't mind me asking?"

He told me, and my jaw dropped.

"That's a lot of money."

"Some of it was family money, which actually makes it harder for me. Jeremy sold us on Generistic, and he definitely marketed it to us as a cause—honest AI, developed and packaged for good, useful purposes. In a form with safeguards—a tool that regular people could use and feel good about."

"So, what happened then?" I asked, as we walked, both of us pausing occasionally for Biga to do his thing. "It sounds like something went wrong."

He sighed. "Jeremy took our money. Then he also got the backing of some very important people in Silicon Valley. People who could give more money as well as their powerful endorsements to the company. Their involvement changed everything. Steve and I didn't matter anymore.

Jeremy would nod his head and listen to us, then do exactly what his new powerful backers told him to do. The whole scope of Generistic's product has changed."

From what I'd heard of Jeremy Bradshaw, this sounded in character. Or about right for his *lack* of character.

"No more 'honest' AI," I said.

Aveer shook his head. "He wanted to provide what other AI companies are offering. He said we'd lose business if we limited the system's capabilities."

I told him about Nate and me overhearing the conversation in The Riverside.

"Now I know that was what Steve Rawlins was talking about, when he yelled at Jeremy," I said. "I also heard since then that Jeremy was caught in a hotel suite in San Francisco with Rawlins's wife."

Aveer stared at me, a look of shock on his face. "Steve didn't tell me about that."

He looked down at the ground, deeply troubled. "This changes things. I wanted to talk to you because my friend and I have been deceived. Now that I know about Steve's wife, I worry even more for him. On the second to last Saturday of the month, Steve, Jeremy, and I were supposed to meet at The Riverside as usual to talk about Generistic. That afternoon, Steve texted me and told me not to bother coming. He needed to meet with Jeremy by himself. It was about something personal."

GOING across the street to tell the chief what Aveer had told me seemed like tattling.

But after our walk, I told Aveer he should tell the police about this new angle on the case.

Once I got back to the bakery, I was thrown into mind-numbing busyness. Lunch service was about to start, and I didn't have a lot of time to think about Aveer's dilemma. It was Thursday, and the large group of knitters had decided to stay for lunch. On top of that, a group of women who were hiking up at Henry Cowell State Park had decided to eat lunch at the bakery.

Both groups were having a great time. And showed no signs of wanting to leave. We were packed until closing.

But as soon as we shut the door, I grabbed my phone and texted the chief.

Talk soon? News on the case

Everything I'd just learned reinforced our previous conclusion: Steve Rawlins looked guilty as heck. I now knew he had two big reasons to kill his longtime friend: betrayal in both business and friendship. He'd been seen having a public argument with the man. And Bradshaw's body was found a little too close to where that argument had taken place. Now Rawlins was AWOL. Though he had far-reaching responsibilities at work and was also a family man, connected with many people. Wouldn't *someone* know where he was?

Again, I had the feeling Aveer knew more than he was saying.

As THE STAFF and I cleaned the back room and wiped down the dining area and counters, we listened to music— Rose's choice today, a jazz playlist with Ella Fitzgerald and Sarah Vaughn. I wasn't excited about it at first, but the more we listened, the more the music grew on me.

I threw myself into chores that I'd performed so many times I could work on autopilot. Even though I wasn't consciously thinking about the maze murder, my brain was processing the details in the background, sort of like a computer does when it's running a program but allows you to play a video game at the same time.

Around 4 p.m., my phone buzzed in my apron pocket. I pulled it out.

Coming over now with Brad

I let the two law enforcement professionals in the front door, and we took a seat in the dining area. I set out a carafe of coffee with two mugs and cream in case the two needed a late afternoon jolt of caffeine.

"I met with someone today who works at Arrowfind, where Steve Rawlins works." I told them about Aveer and how Jeremy Bradshaw ditched him and Steve for a group of high-profile Silicon Valley tech bros. "Rawlins and Aveer Gulati invested time and a lot of money—and I mean a LOT of money—in Generistic. Then Bradshaw told them their involvement was no longer needed."

"So there's a financial motive here, too," the chief said, pouring himself a cup of coffee. "Rawlins put out a lot of money."

"I wanted you to know about this news," I said, rubbing my eyes. "But you need to talk to Aveer. I told him he needed to come in to talk to you."

"Wait a minute. If Rawlins has a motive, this Aveer guy does, too," Brad said, turning to the chief. "We need to interview him and determine his whereabouts the night of the murder."

They were right, of course. I wanted to say, but Aveer

was a *really nice guy* and didn't seem like he could murder anyone.

Aveer had told me something he didn't have to share, and that information gave him a strong motive for killing Bradshaw.

Aveer and Amy told me the same thing about Rawlins. *He doesn't have it in him to murder someone. He's not that kind of a person. That's just not something he'd do.*

How could you know? If a longtime friend betrayed you unexpectedly—not just in one way but in two—you could react by doing something extreme. Something you'd never in your right mind think of doing.

"Aveer was headed to work in Sunnyvale when I left him. But I believe he'll come in to talk to you," I said. "He's worried about Rawlins."

"We'll see it when it happens," the chief said sardonically, scanning notes on his tablet. "This is a twist that we weren't expecting, and I want to find out more. How can I contact this Aveer? If I don't hear from him today, I'll need to give him a call."

I texted the chief the phone number from Aveer's business card, feeling guilty. He'd told me everything freely and had probably thought it was in confidence.

"Thanks, Gracie," the chief said as he and Brad leaned in to have a conversation.

"No word on test results?" I asked as I got up to head for the back room.

The chief shook his head. "Unfortunately, these things take time, even as our odds of solving the case go down every day. Damn frustrating. We might hear tomorrow."

As I started for the back room, the chief stopped and shook his head in a "what the hell am I doing" way. He pushed his chair back and stood up. He even gave me a smile.

"Gracie, this information could be very helpful. I appreciate you taking the time to tell us. Thank you."

I went back to work, hoping that Aveer would come in and talk with the chief and really hoping he had had nothing to do with Bradshaw's murder.

Chapter Sixteen

FRIDAY, *October 24*

TONIGHT WAS the grand opening of the River Grove Haunted Maze.

From the moment she entered the back room that morning, Rose buzzed with energy.

She was dressed in Goth attire: a long black lace skirt and pointed black boots that didn't look particularly comfortable for all the walking around she'd have to do today.

She wore a black sweater with an applique of a shiny black cat arching its back. Her face was made up with light, almost white, foundation, and her eyes were heavily shadowed with deep blue eye shadow and heavy black eyeliner.

The dark red lipstick and the shading on her cheekbones made her look ominous indeed. She looked more like the late-night horror movie hostess Elvira, Mistress of the Night, than the quiet, sweet girl next door she'd been on her first day at The Laughing Loaf.

"Rose, you're scaring me." I smiled at her as I passed by on my way to the industrial fridge. She was slicing beignet dough with a big knife. With her new look she could have been a goth axe murderer.

"Gracie, that's the *idea*," she said, her girlish voice sounding strange coming out of a fortysomething female vampire. "Peony told everyone working tonight that we need to dress like we live in the Haunted Maze. She doesn't want anything to take away from the creepy vibe. 'We're all actors when we're at the maze,' she told us. 'We have to stay in character for this to work.'"

Maeve called out from her spot at the oven, where she was checking on sourdough loaves, "I think the fact that there's already been a murder in the maze gives it its creepy vibe. No costume's going to work better than that."

Maeve was right. For certain attendees, anyway.

Mayor C had ordered cupcakes for tonight's maze staff. Beck had been working on these, partly at home, and partly when she got some time at the bakery. She was yawning again, which made me wonder how late she'd been staying up the past couple of nights.

But she'd finished the cupcakes and they were laid out on trays ready to be taken over to the maze tonight.

Instead of going for a scary look—not Beck's style—she'd gone for whimsical. Puffy white ghosts hovered over a night sky of black frosting covered by tiny white stars. A girl witch in a pointed hat that was too big for her leaned forward on her broomstick, preparing to zoom through the sky. And my favorite: an adorable Frankenstein monster with one leg lurching forward on a bright orange background.

"I love these," I said, admiring her detailed work. "But please tell me you actually got sleep last night."

She stifled a yawn. Her cheeks looked rosy, as if she'd just awakened from a nap.

"Much better. I only worked till 9:30 p.m. These were so much fun to make it was hard to stop." She brought out a pink box and opened it to show me eight decorated cupcakes. "And these are for The Laughing Loaf staff. I wanted everyone here to have one."

"They're adorable," I said, thinking I should estimate the time she spent making these and sneak compensation into her paycheck. "What a thoughtful thing to do, Beck."

About an hour into our lunch service, I went up front to check our bread count. Mostly requests for wraps and buttery brioche, though I was happy to see the harvest loaves and rye catching on. I went to the back room, and Maeve and I prepared a tray to take up front. Daisy and Elise were working the lunch line today. In support of tonight's maze opening, Daisy was dressed like a scarecrow and Elise like the Mad Hatter from Alice in Wonderland.

At 4:30 p.m., since it was Friday, Maeve left to drive up to Napa to do her weekend shift at *Pain Parisienne*.

"Goodbye, y'all," she said gaily in an exaggerated combination of a Southern and an Irish accent as she tossed her apron in the laundry bin. "Sorry to miss opening night, Rose, but I'm going to catch it next week with Mayor C. I absolutely love a good scare."

The thought had been popping back into my head, throughout the day.

I needed to talk to Rose.

I kept coming back to this, but I hadn't followed up on it.

Rose had been stationed at the table in front of the maze that whole night of the murder. In fact, she'd been the only one there. The police had talked to her, but I hadn't.

I didn't get time with her until after closing, since she was on the espresso machine most of the day. When she walked into the back room after we locked the front door, I asked if I could pick her brain for a few minutes.

We went into the dining area to sit down. I brought water bottles for us, since I knew it had been a busy day for both of us.

"Rose, I wanted to talk to you about last Saturday night."

Her eyes widened. "Is there any more news?"

"No, unfortunately." I handed her a water bottle and opened mine and took a gulp. "You were there by yourself for a while before Nate and I came out of The Riverside."

"Yes. Everyone else had taken off. Even Mayor C and Peony. So I put in my earbuds and listened to music and started putting makeup and costumes away."

"You may not have heard anything, but think back. Did you see anything going on in the area? Anybody else walking through the green space? "

Rose closed her eyes as if she were visualizing it. "Let me think. I remember someone getting out of their car in The Riverside parking lot. Just in the corner of my eye. But that's just what it's like at The Riverside. It's a bar and people come and go till really late."

I nodded. "Any idea of the type of car? Was it a pickup? A sedan? Compact car?"

"A smaller car. Yeah, like a compact. It looked silvery, shiny, under the lights," she said, closing her eyes for a moment to try to picture it. "Something like that."

"What time would this have been? How soon before Nate and I came out of The Riverside?"

She raised an eyebrow. "Maybe ten minutes or so? I

think. I got a text right before that. Oh, wait a minute. I can check." She pulled her phone out of her apron pocket.

"My friend texted me at 8:42. I noticed the person in the parking lot right before that."

"That's super helpful. Thank you, Rose." Both of us got up and headed to the back room to get going with prep.

I didn't know if this info would help. Rose was right; people did come and go till very late at The Riverside.

I was only interested in one of them.

"If you're just about finished here, Beck, I can take the cupcakes in my car. I'll follow you over and help you unload your cake at The Riverside."

Beck looked up from twisting a tie on a plastic bag of cut bread. She let out a relieved sigh.

"That's so nice of you. It would be a big help."

In fifteen minutes, I carried the trays of cupcakes out to my car, then I took the heavy cake box out to her car in the alley.

I locked up the bakery, though when I was done, I'd still have to come back and get my little dog. I felt guilty leaving him by himself, but when I poked my head into his room, he was curled up asleep on his blanket.

Beck turned into the side parking area at The Riverside. I parked right behind her and went over to help her carry her cake and tools.

I looked across at the maze. As daylight dimmed, lights had turned on, highlighting the huge structure.

"Maybe I'm a little sad to miss it," Beck admitted as she opened her car door and stepped out. "I know Sam wants to see it. He said he wants to go with Nate and Brad sometime before Halloween. It's just not my thing."

"It's not for everyone," I said. "I still feel creeped out after what I saw the other night."

Beck carried the bag of tools and decorations up to The Riverside's secret side door, which led into the kitchen. She used the key to open it, then propped open the door.

Beck and I lifted the cake carrier from the back hatch of her car and carried it into the kitchen. I can tell you, four twelve-inch layers, with frosting and filling, is heavy.

"Beck! And Gracie," Chef Jorge called out when he saw us. "We've cleared your space. Right here." He gestured toward a clean countertop, smiling. "I'll bring you the display case from the storeroom when you're ready."

With dinner service in process, the kitchen was busy and noisy, with staff coming in to get dishes for customers. Orders were called out, pots and pans clashed, mixers turned on, and timers beeped.

Beck looked dazzled by it all and also very excited. As I saw her make her way to the workspace and pull out her tools and decorations, I felt like I was launching her into the world. Maybe the equivalent of what a parent feels dropping their child off at college.

"Beck, take a picture when it's assembled," I said as I gave her a quick hug.

"Thank you, Gracie," she said, hugging me back. "I'll see you tomorrow morning."

As I left, I saw Reggie come into the kitchen and eagerly head for Beck.

Somebody was *very* excited to see his birthday cake.

I went back to my car to get the cupcakes for the maze volunteers. A short Dr. Frankenstein strolled past me, his green face lit up by the glow of his phone.

"Hey, Aiden!" I called out. "Can you help me carry cupcakes over to the table behind the maze?"

He turned around, startled.

"Wait! How did you know it was me?"

We each picked up a tray and walked it over to the table at the back of the maze.

Then I went around to the entrance of the maze to find Rose.

Maze attendees, a lot of them teenagers, streamed down the street in our direction, headed for the green space. Given that the maze was opening in a half an hour, I was surprised it wasn't more crowded. Either Mayor C's Q&A hadn't been as successful as I thought, or attendees were waiting for it to be completely dark to enjoy their haunted maze experience.

I walked over to Rose's table where she was putting the finishing touches on a female zombie's hollowed out eyes. A cold wind had started up, and Rose set down her makeup brush to wrap a scarf around her neck.

"Hey, Gracie," she called cheerfully. "I saw Beck's cupcakes go by. I can't wait to get one. They look amazing."

"You almost done with the makeup?" I asked.

"Just finishing with Lindsey here. I was thinking of going in and taking a tour myself," she said. "Since it's early and not super crowded yet. I haven't been in the maze since . . . well, since we found the body."

I looked at the maze entrance. I had a flashback to finding Jeremy's body a few nights ago and the uncomfortable feeling of being trapped with it.

Maybe what I saw tonight would jar loose something in my thoughts, remind me of something else I'd seen that night.

"Want some company?" I asked Rose. She nodded, as

Lindsey the teen zombie stood up and headed for the part of the maze she was assigned to.

"I admit, I'm scared," Rose said. "I work here and I haven't even been through the whole maze yet. I don't want to tell anyone that. And I've been sitting out here every night in front of it."

"Maybe it won't be so bad if we go through together?" I asked, as a shiver of fear ran through me.

"Okay, Gracie." She took a deep breath and stood up. She closed up her makeup case with a decisive snap.

"Let's do it."

Chapter Seventeen

FRIDAY, *October 24*

WE WALKED over to join the line near the maze entrance, an area lit with eerie green lights. Most of the attendees around us were teens and young adults.

I noticed Deputy Lyle Scoggins standing guard outside the maze.

Amelia Gruber stood at the entrance next to the creepy clown, taking tickets. Her face was plastered with white makeup. She wore a long black gauzy gown and a horned Viking helmet on her head.

"Gracie's my guest," Rose said.

"Oh, my god, Gracie! I'm so glad you came. Now's a good time," Amelia said cheerfully. "Looks like we're getting a few more people than we thought tonight." She looked past to the line forming behind us. I was surprised to see that it had grown and was now winding back to the sidewalk leading into the green space. "Have fun, you guys!"

Slowly, Rose and I entered the first stretch of the maze, with walls covered with spider webs and the big creepy spider that had inspired my *Lord of the Rings* nightmare.

I kept my left hand on the wall next to me, making sure we didn't get lost. I did have to get back to my little dog, and I was starting to feel guilty that I'd left him back at the bakery.

I looked above to see a spider stretched across the top of the maze, leering down over us with green, light-up eyes. One of his legs was motorized, so as you began to pass by, the leg slowly lowered down to take a swipe at you.

Rose and I both let out a shriek, but it was a shriek of fun, us just getting in the spirit of the maze.

I kept my hand on the wall, and we'd need to turn right to keep my hand on it.

"Okay, we're turning here," I said, and we moved into an area lit by eerie purple light. A family of ghosts, actually rather cute ones, dangled in the air above us, swaying to the soundtrack of what sounded like a mournful sea shanty.

Suddenly, a large pirate moved out from behind the group of ghosts and came toward us. He talked in ominous tones about witnessing a mysterious death at sea. When I realized with horror that this was an actual person, I screamed.

Rose leaned toward me and whispered in my ear as she tried not to laugh. "Gracie, I just did his makeup an hour ago. It's Kai Daniels."

I started laughing, and Rose and I both giggled in that uncontrollable way, driven by fear and relief.

"That's okay, Kai. We won't reveal any of your long-lost secrets," I said. "Unless you want us to."

Kai waved to us and blew us a kiss as we continued on.

"Farewell, my dear friends," he called to us in a quavering voice as he went back to his ghost friends.

I kept my hand on the wall of the maze, anchoring myself. I'm glad I did, because I wasn't sure where we were within the maze. The turns, the weird lighting, and the alternating areas of colored light and pitch-black darkness made me feel disoriented.

We continued down the corridor, as glow-in-the-dark skeletons danced under black lights mounted at the top of the maze walls. Suddenly, on either side of us, disembodied hands came out of holes in the walls—bright white bones painted on black gloves to look like boney fingers. They tried, but not too hard, to grab at us.

Rose and I screamed and laughed as we kept moving. I almost forgot to keep my hand on the wall as we moved toward a juncture in the maze. At the last minute, I reconnected with the wall and made sure we turned to the left.

Rose leaned in toward me and whispered. "I think . . . we might be getting close to where we were Sunday night when we found the body."

My heart pounded as she said it, and the memory of that night came back to me.

The turn led us into an area glowing with orange light. Wooden torches had been set up on top of the walls, wrapped round with orange mini lights. They highlighted a cauldron where a real person dressed as a witch, who looked more friendly than scary, stirred a glowing pot while cackling.

The cackle was familiar to me. I tried to figure out who it was.

"Eyeball soup, anyone? It's most delicious. Fresh eyeballs, organic and locally sourced, of only the highest quality." I laughed at her nod to River Grove's health-oriented food culture.

I gazed into the cauldron and saw what had to be grapes, bobbing in a tomato-y broth.

"What this soup needs is some Laughing Loaf sourdough," the witch said, with a fiendish laugh as she brandished her stirring stick.

"Janet!" It was Janet from Clip n' Curl, which didn't surprise me. The short pink curls peeking out from under her witch's hat gave it away.

So far, the maze was more entertaining, and less frightening, than I thought it would be, which was a relief—in the light of the maze murder and the slowing ticket sales this week.

But I felt a sick feeling in the pit of my stomach as I anticipated seeing the spot where we'd found Jeremy Bradshaw.

We continued down the corridor in the dark, with the exception of a movie clip projected on the wall opposite us. It was a black and white clip with an old-timey, flickering effect.

It was Mayor C, gruffly giving the River Rats softball team a pep talk before a game—the final game last season between the River Rats and the Los Gatos Gopher Trappers.

You will go out there to win. All of you. You have what it takes. I am sending you on a mission tonight to beat the Gopher Trappers. Go out and . . . DESTROY THEM!!!

.   .   .

SOMEONE HAD PUT an echo effect and pitch shift on the last sentence of the mayor's pep talk, so her voice suddenly deepened into a supervillain roar. Big, telescoped eyes appeared, superimposed over the mayor's eyes.

It was terrifying and hilarious—and Rose and I couldn't stop laughing.

After a few minutes of giggles, Rose and I moved on. The lights dimmed until a spotlight appeared on a figure directly in front of us.

There, in all his creepy glory, was Zombie Runty.

Shadows appeared on Runty's face, so his cheeks looked sunken in. A gash across his forehead revealed a glimpse of what looked like brains, probably Rose's handiwork. In one hand, he carried a bloodied softball bat.

We jumped when Zombie Runty moved toward us.

"Hello, ladies. Welcome to my dugout. Care to watch the game with me? Who's gonna give me that good ol' Runty cheer?"

I tried to figure out who this was, and I shot a look at Rose, who shrugged.

We were still a little frightened, so we did a weak, half-hearted Runty cheer: *Run-ty Run-ty Run-ty"* while doing the accompanying clap and stomp, the standard warm-up cheer at River Rats softball games.

"That's weak sauce, guys," Zombie Runty commented with a groan, unimpressed.

I immediately knew who this was. Our old friend, River Grove High class clown, Sky Robbins.

We moved on down the corridor, and I quickly reached my hand out to the wall to keep us on track as we turned the corner.

As we walked, my phone lit up with a message: Nate

texting with an interesting bird call he wanted to share with me before our talk later.

I glanced at it, then went to slide it into my jacket pocket. As I did, the light glinted off something on the ground near the right maze wall. I held my phone over the spot and saw it again.

I pulled a tissue out of my purse and wrapped it around my fingers as I picked the metallic piece up.

It was a Corner Market keychain.

Chapter Eighteen

Friday night, *October 24*

"What did you find?"

Rose stared down at the keychain. "I heard you say somebody worked there. Who was it?"

"Michael Muller. The victim's brother-in-law."

I looked around us. A group of teens were approaching Zombie Runty after watching the mayor's clip. They laughed almost uncontrollably.

"Let's move on," I said, as I glanced ahead. "From what you remember, Rose, is this the area we were in when we found the body?"

"A few feet ahead," she said. "That alcove at the turn."

I needed to get back to the bakery and my little dog, so I couldn't spend much more time here.

I kept my hand on the wall, and we continued until the theme of the maze changed to something more whimsical and lighthearted.

"We're getting into the kids' area," Rose said. "Not

scary, more a place where parents with young kids can come in a side entrance and avoid the intense stuff."

Lighthearted music played, and a line of jack-in-the-boxes appeared. Ghosts, witches, and vampires took turns popping out of their boxes.

We rushed past, as a teen wearing a witch costume handed us fun-sized candy bars from her cauldron.

Not long after, we exited the maze into an area with large pumpkins and giant papier mache toadstools. Another area designed for small children. There were a handful of young grade schoolers here, dressed in their Halloween costumes. A Disney princess and a superhero, and a couple of animals—a cow and a fox—wearing cute, homemade costumes.

Rose looked at the line forming back at the entrance.

"I've got to get back to my table," she said. "I'm on call if anyone needs a touch-up on makeup or a costume fix."

"Thanks for getting me in, Rose. I'm glad I was able to see it on opening night. It was less scary than I thought."

Just then, my phone buzzed. I had a text from Beck, with a picture of her birthday cake for Reggie—sitting at the end of the long dining table in The Riverside. The cake looked beautiful, of course, and the scenario of kids on the bench in a park looked lifelike and whimsical.

Then I noticed the five elderly men, including Reggie, lined up right behind the cake in the same order. Grownup versions of the boys on the bench.

> Reggie's friends are laughing at how much they look like the kids on the cake.

> They all love it!!!!

Beck followed this with another excited text.

OMG!!!!!!!

Reggie just said he can put me on retainer
as The Riverside's cakemaker! He'd pay
me a salary every month to do work for him
and The Riverside.

This didn't surprise me. Beck would be a great resource to have on hand to do cakes for Reggie's events, and any weddings, engagement parties, birthdays, or work events held at The Riverside.

I texted back.

Congratulations, Beck! Let's talk soon. I
want to hear what you're thinking.

I felt happy for Beck, but then there was an unsettled feeling deep in me that change was coming.

I knew it was good.

But it was still change.

I walked back to my car in The Riverside lot. I hoped my pup was okay back at the bakery. I felt for the keychain in my purse.

The keychain could mean nothing. It might have been Michael's. Or anyone who'd gone through the maze who worked for the store. Or anyone who'd even shopped there.

But finding it in the area where Jeremy had been killed also had a good chance of *not* being a coincidence.

Chapter Nineteen

Friday, *October 24*

By the time I got back to The Laughing Loaf, it was dark. The alley was empty and silent.

It felt scarier right now than the haunted maze.

I parked, then sped up the steps to check on the poor pup I'd left alone for almost an hour. A cold wind whipped past me, penetrating my down jacket as if it were made of light cotton.

As I worked the key in the lock, I didn't notice the big, sleek sedan parked not far from the steps.

Biga had been curling up on his blanket. He eagerly came over to lick my hands.

As I sat in the pen holding Biga, a loud knock on the door startled me.

Maybe it was seeing the maze tonight and reliving finding the body a few nights ago. Or maybe it was the dark outside and the leadup to Halloween. And all the talk of murder this week.

The knocking continued.

My heart pounded.

Had someone lurking at the maze followed me back to the bakery, guessing I'd be alone?

I picked up my phone and checked my texts and calls.

Besides Beck's excited texts from earlier, there was one phone call.

It was from an unidentified number. My phone hadn't listed it as a spam call.

I pressed to listen to the voicemail. It was a man speaking in a raspy voice, with a slight southern accent:

"Gracie, this is Steve Rawlins. I need to talk to you. Aveer told me you were someone I could trust. I have some things to say, but I'm not ready to talk to the police."

Sweat broke out on my forehead. My stomach started to twist uncomfortably.

He sounded like a man preparing to confess.

If he were to talk to the chief, chances are he'd be arrested on the spot. Big surprise, the chief wasn't always a great listener.

So Rawlins had come to me. Where was Aveer?

While I considered this, the tapping on the door continued.

I sent a text back to the number.

Is Aveer with you?

I didn't feel comfortable talking to our number one suspect unless there was someone else here. With the fear that was taking hold of me, I worried that maybe Aveer had set this up as a trap. Maybe he'd been in on Bradshaw's murder all along. He'd also been screwed by the AI entrepreneur. Maybe the two of them had killed Bradshaw together.

Did I trust Aveer?

I trusted him more than I trusted Rawlins.

Three dots hovered as Rawlins typed, then:

He's here

I responded:

I want to see you both at the door

I heard another knock. I approached the window to check.

Rawlins stood back from the door. He seemed very tall next to Aveer, who was shivering without a jacket. My friend from the Indian restaurant flashed me a warm smile.

I unlocked the door and let them into the back room.

Rawlins looked like he had in the photos I'd seen online. But thinner and bonier, as if the stresses of this week had taken their toll. There were shadows under his eyes, and he looked like he hadn't shaved in a while.

"Let's go up to the dining area and sit," I said. We sat at a table away from windows, and I kept the lights low. I didn't want the chief or anyone else in the know to walk by and see that the fugitive Steve Rawlins was sitting here chatting with me.

My first instinct was to offer the two men something to drink or eat. But I was tired after a long day. I had zero energy for hospitality.

Aveer spoke first.

"Gracie, I told Steve about our conversation earlier this week, and he wants to tell you his story."

Rawlins sighed and sat back in the chair. "It's been a long week. A month ago, I hired a private detective to follow Shayla. She'd been acting oddly. Said she needed to stay late for work. The next week, she wanted to check out a Pilates class and needed me to pick up Andrew, our son, from a friend's house. I suspected something, so I had the detective follow her when she said she was going shopping up in the city with a friend. The detective brought back photos of Bradshaw getting romantic with my wife in a hotel suite."

"I'm so sorry," I said. "Did you confront Shayla about it?"

"I went to Bradshaw first. Aveer and I were Generistic investors, and we had a meeting scheduled at The Riverside Sunday night." He rubbed his eyes. "We had a lot to talk about, since Bradshaw had just told us he was taking Generistic in a new direction. Bradshaw told us our advice was no longer needed. He'd hooked up with some high-profile Silicon Valley investors who wanted to partner with him—"

"Aveer told me about this," I broke in.

Rawlins shook his head and continued.

"I told Aveer to sit this meeting out. I needed to talk to Bradshaw one-on-one, on a personal matter."

Rawlins' eyes watered up. "I took my gun with me as I headed up to River Grove. I had never been so angry in my life. Up until the moment I got out of my car in The Riverside parking lot, I was ready to kill Bradshaw. I had a gun with me. And I had a couple of good reasons." He looked down at the table as his voice got thin and quiet. "I came so close. I never thought I could do something like that."

I listened as Rawlins described sitting with Bradshaw, telling him what he'd done—some of which Nate and I had overheard that night.

He slumped down in his seat. "The thing is, Bradshaw said I'd done this to myself. Pushing Shayla away. He was right. We were dealing with some medical issues with our son. I was not there for her."

"My boyfriend and I heard the argument, Steve. We heard what he said to you. We saw you walk out. Then we saw Bradshaw sit there laughing to himself."

Rawlins stared at me. "So you were there."

"Where did you go after you left The Riverside?" I asked.

"Shayla texted me. She wanted to get together and talk. So I headed to a restaurant in Palo Alto to meet with her. It turned out to be a very good meeting. Great, actually." He widened his eyes as if he was still surprised by it.

"You turned your gun over to Chief Westerman the day afterwards," I said. "Did you have another gun by any chance?"

Rawlins shook his head.

"The gun you handed over didn't shoot the bullet that killed Bradshaw," I said. "The chief knows this now."

Rawlins looked at me as if he didn't understand what I was saying.

"It was rifle ammunition," I said, watching realization dawn in his eyes. "You should tell the chief your arrival time at the restaurant where you met Shayla, and the name of the place. And please go in to talk to him. I don't think you have anything to be afraid of."

Rawlins stood up and reached out to shake my hand, which felt strangely corporate.

"Thank you, Gracie. I'll talk to him tomorrow." He nodded slowly. "I'm glad Aveer told me to see you."

I was so tired right now, I could fall asleep standing up. As we headed for the back door, I passed Biga's pen. He was curled up on his bed, asleep. Probably exhausted by our high step count this week.

With a wave back at me, Rawlins went out the back door, heading for his car.

Aveer paused on the step and turned to look up at me.

"You said you have a boyfriend,"

"I do," I said. I saw the glow in his eyes dim just a bit. "He's a good guy."

He gave me a shy, sad smile.

"And you're an amazing woman, Gracie."

I still hadn't found River Grove's latest killer, but it felt good to hear those words.

Chapter Twenty

Friday night, October 24

Total step count for Friday: 15,410

After Rawlins and Aveer left, I was faced with a choice.

Go home and get some sleep.

Or text the chief and tell him about the conversation I'd just had with his missing suspect.

I decided to text him. If he got back to me, I'd talk to him tonight and tell him everything Rawlins had told me.

If the chief didn't get back to me, I could put Biga in his crate and go home and get some sleep.

> I just talked to Steve Rawlins. He came to the bakery.

> And I found something in the maze

My phone rang within 30 seconds.

"What the hell's going on, Gracie? Where are you?"

"I'm at the bakery. Wanna talk?"

I heard him yawn. "I was doing security duty at the maze. Give me five minutes."

When he appeared at the back door, I let him in.

"Decaf?" I asked.

"Sure."

I went to make him a drip decaf and myself some mint tea. By the time I got back to the table with our drinks, the chief was planted in his seat, scrolling through something on his tablet.

I passed him his mug and took a seat.

"Rawlins came by with a mutual friend. He wanted to tell his story."

"Why did he go to you?" He lifted his hands in frustration. "I've been trying to get hold of the guy all week. What did he say that was so important?"

I told him what Rawlins had said—with as much detail as I could. How he'd wanted to kill Bradshaw for ditching his help with the startup and for stealing his wife. But he couldn't make himself do it.

"He left to meet with his wife at a restaurant in Palo Alto. It sounds like they're trying to work through this. Rawlins wants to tell you everything. Tomorrow if you can do it."

"You really don't think he killed Bradshaw." He looked over at me. He'd dug his heels in on this case, and I don't think he wanted to give up what he'd been insisting on all week.

"I don't think there's any evidence that he killed him. You must have suspected that."

He tilted his head noncommitallly and leaned back in his chair.

"Okay." He changed the subject. "You said you found something in the maze tonight."

I took the wrapped keychain out of my pocket and laid it on the table.

"I found this near the spot where we found Bradshaw's body. It's a Corner Market keychain. I'm not sure what it means or who it belongs to."

The chief gave it a passing glance and snorted. "Anyone could have dropped it."

Then he looked straight at me as I watched him process this.

"Michael Muller works there," he said. "I've seen him when I've gotten coffee in the mornings."

He pulled out a plastic bag and carefully took the wrapped keychain, slipped it into the bag, then sealed the top shut.

"I asked Amy Bradshaw whether Michael understood all the bad stuff Bradshaw had been doing. She said, 'Michael knows a lot more than we all think he does.' But when I suggested he might have gone after Bradshaw, she stopped talking to me."

The chief let out a short laugh. "Well, what did you expect? And you say *I'm* blunt, Gracie."

"Yeah, but my point here is, Michael does work at the Corner Market."

"Anyone could have dropped that. Dylan Delgado did some work on the maze construction. Maybe it was his."

"What if you checked for *fingerprints*?" I asked sweetly.

"I'm not sure it'll get us anywhere, but I'll do it."

We sat in silence for a few minutes, both of us close to falling asleep.

"What do you do when your main suspect is no longer your main suspect?" The chief asked, rubbing his forehead and closing his eyes.

"You continue down the list and look at the other people with motives. How about Candace and Tom Muller?"

"Come on, Gracie." The chief shook his head. "Those two? I can't imagine either one of them pulling off something like that."

I was skeptical. "Powerful emotions come up when someone hurts your child." I thought about my calm, reserved dad's anger at my ex-husband when he found out Ben had threatened to tell the FBI I was selling secrets with him. "Maybe you should talk to them again."

The chief looked at me, then grunted. He typed more notes into his tablet.

"Thanks for the damn to-do list."

Chapter Twenty-One

SATURDAY, October 25

Total step count for Saturday: 11,210

THE DAY STARTED OUT WELL.

At 10 a.m., my phone buzzed with a text from the chief.

> Steve Rawlins just left.

> He was upfront and answered all my questions. Did not arrest him.

I chuckled that he felt he had to tell me that.

Steve Rawlins had kept his word and explained his story, and I was relieved.

Another text:

> Fingerprints on keychain are a match for Michael Muller.

This sobered me, as I thought about the Mullers' son. Of course, as the chief said last night, the keychain being found near the murder site might not prove anything.

When Mayor C came into the bakery at 9:30, she seemed more upbeat than I'd seen her in a week.

"How did the maze opening go last night?" I asked her as I entered her order into the system. "I went through with Rose and really enjoyed it. Scary but also funny. Zombie Runty was hilarious."

Mayor C laughed nervously. "I wasn't a fan of the film clip of me. But the teens convinced me the attendees would enjoy it." She tapped her card on the point-of-sale system to pay for her order. "We had eighty-two visitors last night, Gracie. That's higher than I expected."

"I didn't see many younger kids, but maybe that shouldn't have been the target audience anyway."

The mayor frowned. "I think you're right. The teens and young adults last night more than made up for the lack of young families."

I was curious as I thought about my journey through the twists and turns of the maze last night. My trick of consistently keeping my hand on the wall helped, for the most part. But the maze itself was challenging—it had been designed to specifically confuse attendees.

"Corinne, who designed the maze? I don't mean the decorations and effects. But who planned out the maze structure itself? It seemed more intricate than your typical Halloween maze."

The mayor looked up at me as she put her credit card away.

"I never got the name," she said, zipping up her bag. "Some retired guy. Peony handled that. She could tell you who."

Reluctantly, I made a note to stop by City Hall to see my nemesis later that day.

A LITTLE AFTER closing at 2:45 p.m., I had a few minutes to spare. I took Biga outside. He really needed it, and I didn't want to clean up any of his messes because I'd put it off too long. He was happy to be outside, and, once he'd done his business, he was even happier to bark an urgent warning at a squirrel scampering up a tree on the other side of the cars in the alley.

"Thanks, he deserved that, Biga Boy. Glad you're looking out for us." He seemed happy to accept the praise, so I rubbed his head and he pressed into my leg lovingly.

I decided I'd go over to chat with Peony now. I wasn't excited about it, but my question was simple and shouldn't take too long.

I texted Peony.

> I have a maze question. Can you meet me out back? I've got my dog with me.

In a few minutes, I received her reply. She seemed miffed at me for requesting some of her precious time.

> Oh my God.

> Fine.

I walked down the alley to Loudon Way, then took the sidewalk up to the street, passing Gordon Dabney and the mayor who were outside City Hall's green door, probably reveling in last night's success.

I went around to the back door. Peony was leaning languidly against the stair rail, drinking a can of diet coke.

"Good afternoon, Peony. Great job on the maze by the way."

"Uh, okay." She flashed a suspicious look at me. "Thanks?"

"I had one question. Something I was curious about. Who designed the maze structure?"

Peony looked at me as if she were trying to figure out how to deny me the information.

She sighed. "It was some old math teacher. Tom Muller. He said mazes were his thing."

I nodded calmly as my heart began to pound.

"Okay, thanks, Peony," I said, then tugged on Biga's leash and backed away to leave.

"That's it?" She stood up, grumbling under her breath. "Oh, my *God*. You could have texted that and saved me the trouble of coming outside in the cold."

"Have a great afternoon," I said with a smile and cheerful wave, as I headed around the building toward the street to get back to my bakery.

A FEW MINUTES LATER, Biga and I were in the alley.

I noticed a car parked by the back door to Loudon's Antique Emporium. I assumed it was the developer who'd bought the property.

When a nicely dressed couple came out of the back door, I greeted them and introduced myself.

"I'm Gracie Markley, and I own The Laughing Loaf." We smiled and shook hands. "I was wondering how your process is going with renovating the space."

"Oh, we've heard of you, Gracie," the woman answered, with a knowing smile at her partner. "Your bakery was what interested us in this building in the first place. We think downtown River Grove is primed for growth, thanks to what you've done with your bakery. We're hoping to open a few retail stores in this building. There's a lot of renovation and earthquake retrofitting ahead of us—"

"And an awful lot of clean out," the man interrupted with a sardonic roll of his eyes.

"But we love the historical importance of Loudon's. It may take us a while, but we think Loudon's, along with your bakery, can be the start of a downtown renaissance in River Grove."

"What's your timeline?" I asked her, as I saw Biga sniffing at a discarded fast food bag in the alley.

"Now that we own the building, we'll start cleanout soon and renovation in the new year. We'll begin leasing units once our architect comes up with a design and mockups."

"I know someone who might be interested. She does high-end cake design. She's a current employee of mine who's considering starting her own business. If she does want to pursue this, she'd be the one to talk to."

"Her business could fit in well here," the woman said. "We'd be interested in talking to her, after the start of the new year." She reached into her pocket and pulled out a business card. "My name's Marina Karakas, and this is my partner, Brandon Flynn. Please keep in touch, Gracie."

With a spring in my step, I pulled Biga away from licking something that did not look edible.

I headed inside the back of the bakery, excited about the possibilities. I'd get the information, then pass it on to Beck, since it was her decision how to proceed.

I wanted the best for my assistant manager, but jealously, I wanted her close by.

And next door was pretty close.

I took Biga out for a longer walk later.

After all my walks this week, I found myself feeling out of sorts if I didn't get my steps in. We took the trail along the river. I'd looked at Beck's messages again this morning, especially the photo of her cake on The Riverside's long table.

As I came to the back of The Riverside, I glanced up at the saloon's back balcony and Reggie's conference room window on the second floor.

No sign of the birthday boy. He could be sleeping off last night's party. Or enjoying a late brunch with his friends. Or feasting on the remains of Beck's cake.

After I'd settled Biga back in his pen at the bakery, I stepped out into the back room, where Beck and Rose were doing prep for Sunday.

Rose was filling pumpkin tart shells, and Beck was pulling my brioche loaves out of the oven and transferring them to the cooling racks. The smell in the room was sweet and buttery, tinged with the tantalizing smell of fall spices.

I checked my harvest loaves in the proofer, inhaling the rich, earthy smell; they were right on schedule. Since I'd have one more Nate-less evening, I might stay later to try a new fall recipe—Volcano Rye. It was a dense, dark rye bread with a short rise and a long, slow bake. It was popular in Iceland, where the loaves were wrapped tightly and slowly baked underground, near a hot spring or volcano. It was hearty and satisfying—a perfect bread for the cool fall weather. My contingent of rye fans would love it.

Nate would love it.

Then it hit me.

Nate.

He'd texted me last night, for his usual check-in and chat.

After everything going on last night—the maze, Steve

Rawlins' story, and my late-night talk with the chief—I'd locked up the bakery, gone home, and fallen asleep.

Now I plunked down on my office chair and pulled out my phone.

> Sorry I didn't call you back last night. I went to the maze. BIG break in the case.

Nate was coming home tomorrow. I was weary from this investigation—which had as many twists as the maze itself.

I thought more about his suggestion that we have a getaway when he got back from this trip. It wasn't like I'd have to worry about leaving the bakery now. It would be in good hands. Many good hands.

Soon my phone buzzed with a response.

> No worries

> Had to ditch another skunk before I could get into my cabin last night. Excited to hear about your breakthrough.

> See you tomorrow night!

Maybe Elana was right; I didn't know how to have fun. I'd put in full days at the bakery, then spent my spare time working on the case. An arrest hadn't been made, but in the light of the meeting with Steve Rawlins, I'd crossed him off my suspect list. I had a couple of possibilities now, and there was a case to be made for either of them.

And the fact that I couldn't stop thinking about it made me realize something.

This *was* my fun.

Chapter Twenty-Two

Sunday, *October 26*

Total step count for Sunday: 15,283

After lunch service that day, the weather turned cold.

Clouds had moved in and were hovering low, threatening to unload a delivery of rain on the town. The air felt heavy with moisture.

Maybe people had stayed home because of that. The dining area was only half filled, and the guests at the tables looked like they'd settled in for a warm, cozy day inside.

With the relief of having delivered what Reggie called the "perfect" cake for his birthday, Beck seemed more relaxed. I caught her yawning a few times, and it looked like she wanted to take a nap. But there was a sleepy smile on her face.

She sang louder to the background music, and when she

was working the front counter, she greeted customers with an extra dose of her considerable cheer.

Since it was a quiet day, I thought I'd attempt a walk home to drop Biga off with my dad. That way I could go directly to Nate's when he got back tonight. I was willing to risk a downpour so I could get a good walk in. And, of course, meet my day's step count goal—for one more entry on my spreadsheet.

"Don't worry about it," Beck said with a smile as she slid another tray of tarts into the oven. "Look what it's like outside. It's gonna be slow till we close. Rose and I can handle anything that comes up."

I took my warm coat off the rack and slid my arms in, tucking my phone into my inside pocket in case anything did come up at the bakery. Then I went to get Biga's jacket on him. I clipped his leash onto his harness, and we headed out the back door.

We'd follow the trail along the river, but in the opposite direction we did when out for our usual walk. Instead of heading past The Riverside and down to the clearing, we'd follow the river, then switch over to the streets once we got closer to our house.

The skies were not looking promising, as the grey layer of clouds above us darkened. I sped up, hoping we'd make it home and beat the rain.

That didn't happen.

While we were still on the river trail, the sky let loose. At first, a few fat drops of rain smacked my face, then the rainfall turned into an onslaught. As gusts of wind picked up, sideways sheets of rain slapped my face. An older couple passed me, bundled in raincoats. They gave me a grim smile and said something I couldn't hear, their words snatched up by the wind.

We were nearing Cannes Way, and the Muller's house, which had a silver Honda Civic parked in the driveway. After Friday's tense talk with Steve Rawlins, our field of suspects had narrowed to two.

Both of them lived in the house we were approaching.

My stomach twisted uncomfortably. I imagined Michael Muller glaring out of his window at me, his lips twisted, his heavy brow furrowed.

I thought back to my talk with the chief. Michael had known how Jeremy Bradshaw had treated his sister and had been angry at his brother-in-law. And according to Candace Muller, he had a gun.

I sped up and, as if he knew we needed to, Biga sped up, too, moving his little legs back and forth faster than I thought possible.

I started jogging, as cold rain lashed at my bare wrists, and wind whipped my wet hair across my face.

I heard a voice, slow and grating, tinged with desperation.

"*Stop now*. Stop right where you are."

I froze in my tracks and turned around to see Tom Muller, wearing a raincoat and aiming a rifle at me. Biga started growling.

Please, Biga! Not now.

Muller might start shooting if he felt on edge and trapped.

There were no witnesses on the trail today, since most people had made sensible decisions to stay inside.

"That must be the gun you used to kill Jeremy Bradshaw," I said, rain dripping from the ends of my hair. "Is it yours or Michael's?"

I saw it now. When Tom felt threatened and thought

the truth was coming out about what he'd done, he was willing to toss his son under the bus.

"Of course, it's Michael's," Tom Muller said, his face twisting in anger. "You've got a track record of getting things wrong, don't you, Gracie? First, you were so sure Steve Rawlins killed Jeremy. Now it's my turn to take the blame. I'm surprised anyone even listens to you in this town."

How did he know Rawlins had been cleared of the murder? Rawlins had only been cleared last night. It bugged me not knowing how he knew. The news had probably jolted Muller—who'd felt safe all week, knowing the circumstantial evidence pointed to Rawlins.

The best chance for me and Biga to get out of this situation was for me to play up my sympathy for a man who'd seen his daughter repeatedly mistreated by Jeremy Bradshaw.

"It must have been hard for you. To see what Amy went through with Jeremy for so long," I said, trying to keep my teeth from chattering from the cold. "She stuck it out for a lot longer than I would have. Seeing her hurting must have been incredibly painful for you and Candace."

"He was a selfish, lying man. A horrible excuse for a human being." I saw him bristle as he thought of his son-in-law. His lip curled as he continued to keep the gun unwaveringly pointed at me. "Amy was too good for him. Talented, beautiful, and always trying her best to forgive that worthless scum. I raised her to have a better life than this. Gymnastics lessons, expensive camps, special coaches, years of investing in her life. All I ever wanted was the best for her. I felt helpless. How could I stop the man from ruining her life? I had to do something."

I felt sorry for him, seeing his grief. But Tom Muller had

no right to take his son-in-law's life. And this hadn't been a spur of the moment decision on his part.

"Tom, I know you designed the haunted maze. And if you planned it out yourself, you'd know exactly where you could leave a body, and how you could escape before it was found. You must have been thinking about this for months."

A faint smile crossed the man's face.

"I enjoyed the challenge," he said, moving further under the dry, sheltered porch overhang, while keeping the rifle trained on me, still out in the rain. I really wished he'd invite me and Biga to join him, so we could get out of the downpour, but that wasn't happening.

"I planned for a spot in the maze that was hidden from the outside entrance but quick to get in and out of. A place where I could kill him and leave him. I knew this had to happen before the maze opened. I didn't want anyone else to get hurt. Just Jeremy."

I continued with my sympathy ploy, though it was sounding like a stretch at this point.

"I'm glad you didn't want to hurt anyone else," I said, with what I hoped was a convincing nod.

"Jeremy had a dinner meeting at The Riverside at 7 p.m., the second to last Saturday of every month. The week before the maze opened. I waited in the parking lot until he came out to his car. I said I needed to talk to him, and it was important. I didn't want anyone to overhear us."

I swallowed. Behind his glasses, Tom Muller's eyes glimmered with quiet satisfaction.

"We went into the maze and once we got to the spot, I fired the gun. He crumpled down but I could see he was still breathing. I'd done my research, but I must have botched my aim," Tom continued, a distant look in his eyes. "I heard voices. A group of people was making their way through. They seemed lost. But I knew the maze well. They wouldn't be able to get to me fast enough. I quickly made my way to the opposite entrance and headed to my car in the parking lot."

That would have been us. Nate, Rose, and I. We'd been that close to coming face-to-face with this unhinged man carrying a gun.

Biga, wet and cold, began whimpering.

"Can I pick my dog up?" I asked weakly. "He's so cold he's shivering." I wanted to justify it with *your grandkids really love my dog.*

Tom Muller thought about this. "Fine. But stay right there." He watched me carefully as I bent down to pick up Biga, his gun still trained on me.

I gathered my dog in my arms and held him close against me, trying to share my body heat with him.

The cold had seeped through my wet clothes and was chilling my bones. All I wanted was to sit down in a warm, dry place.

Then something happened that I couldn't have predicted in a million years.

The front door of the Muller's house opened with a creak. Since Tom was facing me, I saw it before he did.

At the noise, Tom turned around quickly and raised his gun, a look of fear on his face.

Michael Muller stood in the doorway, his eyes narrowed at his father, looking furious. Tom aimed his gun at the doorway, then froze as the reality hit him.

He had almost shot his son.

"You stop that right now," Michael said sternly, like a parent disciplining a toddler.

Tom lay the gun down quickly on the porch, as if it

were hot. It sat there until Michael walked out and picked it up.

"You killed somebody. It's a bad thing to kill people," Michael Muller said, pausing at the front door, a look of utter scorn on his face as he looked at the gun. He calmly turned around and took the gun back into the house.

Tom sat down on the steps. He slumped over, put his head into his hands, and started to sob. In his careful calculations and planning, he'd never imagined it would end this way.

I noticed someone inside, looking out the living room window: Candace Muller, her expression blank and her eyes dry. She showed little emotion as she sat on the sofa watching her husband sob.

She pressed her lips together and got up to leave the room.

I wondered what she'd known. Had she suspected her husband had been involved in their son-in-law's murder?

Maybe, like her son, she knew more than people thought she knew.

As Tom sat with his head in his hands, I called the chief. Five minutes later, he pulled up in the squad car, followed closely by Brad Castro, who wheeled his pickup truck around and parked in front of the Muller's driveway. Both got out and approached the porch cautiously.

"Hey, Tom," the chief called to the man still bent over on the steps. There was an expression on the chief's face I hadn't seen before. It looked like compassion.

"We heard there might be some trouble here and thought we'd come over to see how you're doing."

Michael came out of the front door and sat down on the top step, not far from me. I looked over at him and smiled.

He studied me, and very slowly the muscles in his face softened, as if he was feeling a sense of relief.

"That was a good thing you did, Michael."

"You're okay?" He asked me, keeping a wary eye on his father as the chief and Brad settled in on either side of the man and began questioning him.

"I'm fine. And Biga isn't shivering anymore."

He smiled.

Soon the chief put handcuffs on Tom and read him his rights.

ALL THE EVENTS on my rainy walk happened in a very down-to-earth way. When I stood in front of Tom Muller, I was not particularly scared, though I was worried about my dog. I gave Brad a quick summary of what had happened and what Tom had confessed.

Then I pulled my phone out of my pocket, and with shaking fingers, called my father to come pick Biga and me up.

My father and Mary Jo came by in her orange VW bug, as the chief and Brad led Tom Muller to the back seat of the squad car. Mary Jo got out and immediately rushed to me and Biga, her arms full of towels.

My father even hugged me, which, for a man who wasn't very touchy-feely, was a big deal.

"The maze master did it," he said quietly as he hugged me. "I think you were coming to that conclusion anyway."

Mary Jo handed me one of the dry, warm towels. I wrapped it around Biga and carried him like a baby, which he seemed to like. "I saw tonight that Michael couldn't have killed Jeremy Bradshaw. For years people have gotten him wrong. His father was willing to use that stereotype to save himself."

He nodded. "It sounds like you are right, my dear."

"I was wondering," I said as I prepared to get into the small car. "Do you know anything about tutoring someone for their GED certificate?"

"I've never done it," my father said, frowning as he thought about it. "What made you think of that? Did you have a student in mind?"

He figured it out before I said anything more. He nodded.

"I'll see what I can do. Michael needs somebody on his side. I'll ask at the high school next week when I go to pick up new textbooks," he said.

Not long after, Mary Jo pulled her bug into our carport.

She made me tea and brought me a quilt to wrap up in on the couch, once I'd changed into dry clothes. Biga, still damp, wedged in next to me. I think the two of us slept for an hour.

When I woke up, I checked my phone. I had a steady stream of texts.

From Beck:

> Gracie, where are you?
>
> We thought you were coming right back.
> Let us know!

From Rose:

> B and I getting worried now. We're going to
> call the police!

A later text from Beck:

> Brad called me and said Mr. Muller's been arrested for the murder. OMG!

> So glad you're okay! 🤍🤍🤍🤍

> We love you, Gracie. We'll take care of cleanup and closing. Call me when you can!

Then Nate:

> ETA 5 p.m.

> Your dad called. Coming directly to your house.

So much for our quiet dinner at his house.

I lay back on the couch. Biga raised his head then burrowed back into the quilt.

I called both Beck and Rose to tell them what had happened and that I'd be in tomorrow as usual, bright and early. I dozed off for a few minutes.

I woke up to the sound of my dad opening the door and Nate's concerned voice. I smelled Mary Jo's chicken tetrazzini baking in the oven and realized how hungry I was.

Nate sat down next to me on the couch. He must have seen my face, because he didn't say anything. He sat quietly with me while I told him what had happened today—and all that had happened this week. He listened and held my hand. He cried when he heard what Michael had done.

He didn't ask me questions.

When I was done, he kissed me and told me he was incredibly proud of me.

It was the best gift ever.

Chapter Twenty-Three

Monday, October 27

After I closed and locked the bakery's front door, Beck, Rose, Maeve, and I lurched tiredly through our cleanup and prep.

It had been a crazy and exhausting few days. Business at the maze had picked up quite a bit, after Mayor C's impassioned speech and the introduction of the security plan at the green space Q&A. And of course, the arrest of Bradshaw's killer.

Rose would continue to leave early for the next three days, but after Halloween, the maze would close for good. After helping to disassemble the maze on November 2, with a crew of volunteers that included Nate and me, she'd be back for her full shift at The Laughing Loaf, and we'd be fully covered now after closing.

Whew.

At 4:30 p.m., I looked around for my assistant manager.

I finally found Beck sitting in a seat in the dining area, leaning her head on her hand, a glass of water in front of her.

I slid into the seat next to her.

"Beck, what's going on?" Her face looked pale and her big brown eyes could barely stay open. "Are you okay?"

"Gracie, I know I have a few things to finish up. I'm sorry. But I'm really tired. All I want to do is sleep."

I sighed quietly. "What were you working on last night?"

She looked at me and shook her head. "Nothing. I went to bed at 8 p.m."

I felt bad that my first instinct was to grill her on keeping a strict bedtime.

"Before I went to bed last night, I took a test," she said, her voice shaky. A smile formed on her face. "My mom said I should."

"Wait, what test? What do you mean—"

What kind of detective was I that I hadn't seen this, with all the tiredness? So much for intuition solving a case.

In this case, science did win out over intuition.

Tears welled in her eyes. "I'm pregnant. About seven or eight weeks. But my mom said if I was this tired, that could be why. My first doctor's appointment is next month."

My eyes squinted to keep back the tears, then I decided, what the hell, just let them roll. One of the most amazing people I knew had just received a long-awaited gift. We both sat at the table sobbing to ourselves while smiling. Luckily, the noise was covered by Maeve singing along with Guns n' Roses in the back room.

"Beck," I said through the tears. "I don't know what to say. I am so happy."

Beck's face radiated joy. "I thought it would never happen," she said, her lips trembling. "Just so you know, I'm not telling anyone for another month or so. To make sure."

"I won't say a word. Is Sam happy?"

"He's crazy happy," she said, crying even more while laughing. "Dancing around the house kind of happy. I had to kick him out of our room last night so I could sleep. All he wanted to do was talk about it."

We both laughed. "I am happy for both of you." I thought for a moment. "So let's talk about this, and if you don't feel up for it, we can talk another time. What are you thinking about cake stuff? You've had an offer from Reggie. Are you going to continue with it or slow down for a while?"

"I am for sure taking a break till I get more energy," she said with a yawn. "My mom says the first three months can be hard. I had no idea this was part of being pregnant."

And as an only child, never having seen my mom go through pregnancy, I had no idea either.

We blotted our eyes and took a deep breath.

"What else do you need to do before leaving today, Beck?"

"I'm done—except I need to wipe down the baking tables and stove area."

"Rose and Maeve can do that. Go home now and get some sleep. Celebrate with Sam. He's going to pick you up?"

She nodded and laughed. "I hope so, since he dropped me off."

"Can I tell Nate about this?"

Beck pursed her lips together, thinking. "Let Sam tell him. He can't wait to tell Nate."

"Got it," I said with a smile, standing up. "Please relax tonight, will you?"

She stood up and hugged me and both of us started sobbing again.

As Maeve's voice warbled through an off-key version of "Sweet Child of Mine" in the next room.

Chapter Twenty-Four

Tuesday, October 28

That afternoon, as lunch service was about to end, I came up to the front counter to take over for Beck.

Halloween would be here in three days. I saw more kids and adults coming in during the day in costume. There were superheroes, princesses, kids in creepy rubber masks of political figures, and the most popular in town this season —Zombie Runty.

I must have seen a half dozen teens come in, wearing "blood"-spattered River Rats t-shirts, their faces painted green with blackened eyes.

Now that the maze murder had been solved, the mood in town had lightened. Kids could go out trick-or-treating now, most of them accompanied by parents, of course. Downtown merchants were staying open a few hours later on Halloween to give out treats to the younger kids. I'd delegated that duty to Rose and Maeve, who had planned their costumes and were excited to do it.

I was working at the counter that afternoon, filling pastry orders, when someone came into the bakery who truly scared me.

It was Denise Reyes, Beck's mother.

I tried to figure out why this woman intimidated me so much. She wasn't imposing in any way. She was short, about my height, and in her fifties. With her pale blue eyes and greying light brown hair, she was the opposite of her husband, Felix, who was brown-eyed and olive-skinned, just like Beck.

Today she wore a pastel calico blouse with a Peter Pan collar and a long jeans skirt, which gave her a prim, *Little House on the Prairie* look.

"Good afternoon, Denise." I flashed her a friendly smile. "Good to see you here. What can I get you?"

She nodded. "We're having a nice dinner tonight with the whole family. So I'm here to get several loaves of bread."

Beck's extended family, the Reyes clan, was huge—with three of the sons having wives and at least two kids apiece. Then there were the younger sons, closer to Beck's age, and Beck and Sam. Almost twenty people altogether.

"Will this be a celebration?" I lowered my voice as I said it. I tried to calculate how much bread they'd need for that crew.

"It is," she said, keeping her voice quiet, too. "Though we're not talking about it beyond the family yet. We feel blessed and want to come together to support Beck and Sam."

"I'd say for twenty people you'd need about seven loaves. Today we have harvest loaves, sourdough, some rye loaves, and brioche."

"Is the harvest bread organic?" She asked, frowning.

"Yep. So is the rye and sourdough."

"Give me four harvest loaves, two sourdough, and one rye then." She reached into her large denim bag and pulled out a credit card. She tapped it on the POS system after I entered her order. I gave her an employee discount, since this was really for Beck.

Then Denise gave me a serious look.

"Gracie, I was never in favor of my daughter working here."

Ouch. This wasn't going to be good.

"But in her time here, she has become stronger, more confident." Denise Reyes' eyes misted. "Beck has—well, I believe she has found her calling."

While I processed this completely unexpected comment, Rose headed over with the bagged loaves. I pulled out a large, handled bag and slipped them in.

I lowered my voice.

"Denise, how do you feel about Beck working after having the baby?"

She sighed. "It's not what I would have wanted for her a few years ago. But Beck has changed. She's found something she loves to do. Thank you for giving her that opportunity. And for all those classes. I want her to continue to do what she loves." A sober look crossed her face. "I believe it will make her a better mother."

It made me wonder if she hadn't been given the chance to pursue *her* calling.

"I look forward to hearing what Beck decides for herself," I said, handing her the bag. "This bakery would not be what it is without her. You've raised an amazing young woman."

"God bless you, Gracie." Denise said with a curt nod.

I stood there immobilized for a moment.

Life is full of surprises. People don't often talk about

what makes them change their mind. I didn't think this woman would, especially after hearing her son's opinion about what Beck should do with her future.

After Beck came back to relieve me, I hugged her.

Then I went to lock myself in the bathroom to cry my tears of joy in private.

Chapter Twenty-Five

Saturday, November 1

Step count for the day: 15,421

THE GREEN SPACE in front of The Riverside was full of activity.

A good portion of the town had shown up at 9 a.m. to take down maze decorations, then slowly dismantle the large black panels that made up the maze itself.

The Chamber of Commerce had arranged for a barbecue food truck to park in front of the space. It was a smart move, since the smoky barbecue aroma seemed to be drawing even more volunteers to pitch in with the work.

While Beck and Rose took care of business at The Laughing Loaf, Nate and I worked on boxing decorations from the black panels—to be saved for next year. Peony, who wandered through the green space with a frown and a Mayor C–style clipboard, gave the final word on what was to be kept and what would be thrown out.

After he'd returned from Oregon, Nate had gone through the maze with Sam and they'd both loved it.

"This is like walking through my memories of the maze and reliving it," he said. "Wasn't it about here that Mayor C told us to DESTROY the Gopher Trappers?"

I laughed. "I still don't think the mayor gets why people found it funny."

"I bet she secretly liked it," Nate said. "She'll probably end up using it as a recruiting video for next season's River Rats team."

I snorted. "She might."

"Sam is in full-on dad mode. He kept talking about how cute the kids' portion of the maze was, with all those jack-in-the-box ghosts. He's getting ready."

"I think both he and Beck have been ready for a *long* time."

"Can we volunteer to babysit?" Nate asked, as he rolled up a string of lights from the top of a maze wall.

"We'll have to get in line and take a number. You know how big that family is."

By 11:30 a.m., we'd taken care of one of the longest corridors in the maze, with the help of Janet from Clip 'n Curl and the Key Haus brothers, Victor and Hans.

"I'm hungry," Nate said, turning to me. "Want some barbecue?"

We checked in with Peony, who reluctantly let us take a break, marking something off on her clipboard checklist as if we'd just received demerits for slacking off. Then we walked over to the food truck and ordered. We got our pulled pork sandwiches and sat down on a bench at the edge of the green space.

It was a cold, fall day, but the sun made it feel warmer—

and festive. We were all doing work, but the camaraderie made it feel like a party.

We sat looking out over the slowly shrinking maze. Volunteers had started detaching the black panels, which were being loaded into the back of Jake Daniels' large truck.

Nate turned to me. "Hey, I wanted to ask you, what's the deal with that old-fashioned step counter you're wearing on your belt? That's a real throwback."

"At dinner the night before you left, you said I should get out more, get more exercise," I said, remembering the hurt I'd felt that night. "It sounded like—like you thought I was out of shape."

"What?" Nate looked at me, mortified. "What did I say that made you think that?"

"You said I needed to get outside and get my heartbeat up."

"I said that because being outside is wonderful. It's good for me, it's good for you." He sighed. "You're inside so much. That's *all* I meant. You've got to know there's nothing about you that needs changing. *Nothing.*"

"You mean that?" By the way he looked at me, I was pretty sure he meant it.

"But wait a minute! I want to show you my spread-sheet," I said, fumbling in my bag for my phone. "I tracked my step count every day while you were gone. Did you know I hit 75K steps? That's an average of 10,714 steps a day."

Nate was trying not to laugh. And failing.

He coughed and whispered the words "spreadsheet nerd" under his breath.

Along the sidewalk near The Riverside, not far from us, something caught my attention. Two kids with a chihuahua on a leash. The dog looked a lot like Biga.

Charlie and Luna Bradshaw.

The little dog was feisty, and at times, it looked like it was him taking the kids for a walk. Charlie held the end of the leash, looking like he wasn't sure how to get the dog to stay on the sidewalk.

"Charlie! Stop. Remember what the training book said. You don't let the dog pick where to go."

"But he smells what they're selling at that truck over there."

Luna responded as any older daughter would in this situation. "He can't have it. You know that would be bad for him. Remember, we need to be responsible."

So the Bradshaw kids had gotten their dog.

I told Nate the full story of my visit to the Muller's house with Biga.

"For a little dog, Biga has a big influence on this town." Nate planted a kiss on my lips, then pulled back to wipe a spot of barbecue sauce off my cheek.

I laughed as I watched the two kids run across the green space, chasing their new pet.

"He really does."

THE END

Thank you

Thank you for reading Rye or Die!

If you enjoyed this book, please leave a review or rating on Amazon, Goodreads, or the book review site of your choice.

I truly value the time you take to do this, and it makes my author heart very happy.

Find a typo or inaccuracy?

If you come across any typos or inaccuracies in this book or any of my others, I'd appreciate it if you could let me know using this contact form:

https://victoriakazarian.com/contact

Thanks!

Also by Victoria Kazarian

Drop Dead Bread - Laughing Loaf Mystery #1

Bread to Rights - Laughing Loaf Mystery #2

Trouble You Don't Knead - Laughing Loaf Mystery #3

Sourdough & Cyanide - Laughing Loaf Mystery #4

Proof of Death - Laughing Loaf Mystery #5

An Oven Beyond - Laughing Loaf Mystery #6

Shot Through the Tart - Laughing Loaf Mystery #7

Naan the Wiser - Laughing Loaf Mystery #8

Coming in summer 2026:

Ciabatta Watch Out - Laughing Loaf Mystery #10

Stop, Drop and Rolls: LL prequel novella

Gingerbread and Left for Dead: LL short holiday mystery

Traditional mystery - writing as VL Kazarian

Swift Horses Racing – Silicon Valley Murder Book 1

Across the Red Sky – Silicon Valley Murder Book 2

A Tree of Poison – Silicon Valley Murder Book 3

About Victoria Kazarian

Victoria Kazarian lives and writes in San Jose, California. After working for years as a Silicon Valley marketing professional, she taught high school English and actually owned a bread bakery of her own called The Laughing Loaf. When she's not writing, she enjoys baking artisan breads and forcing her children and dog to go on road trips to the Pacific Northwest.

See what she's up to at victoriakazarian.com

You can contact Victoria—or perhaps leave a message for Gracie Markley herself—at TheLaughingLoaf@ gmail.com

Acknowledgments

River Grove's maze was inspired by the times my childhood friends and I took over my family's garage in Auburn, Washington, and turned it into a haunted house. Leading our friends and neighbors through the spooky "horrors" we dreamed up was a lot like telling a story.

I could not have put this book out into the world without the help of my beta readers: Chris Anderson, Faye Friesen Myers, Amanda Giles, Kerry Nozicka, and Karen Bowers. Thank you for spotting the tricky continuity and timeline issues and for having a heart for this series and its characters. And proofreaders Karen Stevenson, Mary Ann Askins, and Vivian Gudan—thank you for putting your eagle eyes to work on behalf of this book. You have a gift that I do not have!

Thanks to my editor, Honest Magpie (aka Armen), a great resource for structural edits and also for helping me toss ideas around.

Thanks to the Sisters in Crime community, especially the Coastal Cruisers and NorCal chapters, for the support, camaraderie, and great write-ins.

Lastly, thank you to my husband, Pete, for his support and willingness to eat large quantities of takeout food throughout the writing of this book.

Laughing Loaf Bakery Recipes

Volcano Rye

Harvest Loaf

Bucatini Alla Amatriciana

Volcano Rye (Rúgbrauð)

Time needed: about 2 hours

This is a no-yeast bread, popular in Iceland, where they wrap up the dough in a pan, dig a hole in the ground near a hot spring or volcano, and bake it there at low heat for 12 to 24 hours. Don't worry—you don't need to find a local volcano! A long bake in the oven will do the trick.

Volcano Rye (Rúgbrauð)

The bread is nutty and slightly sweet and does not have an overpowering rye flavor. Tastes great toasted and spread with butter or with cream cheese and topped with smoked salmon.

You'll need:
4-1/2 cups rye flour (medium or dark rye)
2 teaspoons sea salt (or <u>non-iodized</u> table salt)
1 tablespoon baking powder
3/4 teaspoon baking soda
2 cups buttermilk
2/3 cup honey
1/3 cup molasses
A pullman loaf pan (with a slide-on lid) OR a 9-inch loaf pan.

Preheat the oven to 325°F with a rack in the center position.

Get out two bowls: one larger one for dry ingredients and a smaller one for wet ingredients.

In the large bowl, whisk together the flour and salt. Then sift in baking powder and baking soda (to prevent any little chunks or lumps).

In the "wet" bowl, mix together the buttermilk, honey, and molasses.

Pour the wet ingredients into the dry ingredients, then stir to combine.

Pour the batter into a lightly greased 9-inch pullman pan. Wet your fingers, then smooth over the top of the loaf. Lightly grease the lid and slide the lid onto the pan.

If you don't have a pullman loaf pan, you can also use a regular loaf pan 8-9 inches long. After filling the pan, wrap it in aluminum foil. Place the wrapped pan on a baking sheet in the middle rack of the oven to bake.

Bake the bread for 1 hour and 40 minutes. Turn off the oven and remove the lid (or aluminum foil) from the pan. Leave the loaf in the turned-off oven for another 10 minutes, then remove from the oven and turn the loaf out of the pan onto a cooling rack.

Cool the loaf completely before slicing.

You can store the leftover bread tightly wrapped at room temperature for several days. Freeze for longer storage.

Harvest Loaf

Total Time needed: 4 hours, 15 minutes
This is a delicious multigrain bread with a soft and fluffy inside. It's great for sandwiches or breakfast toast.
You can also add your favorite seeds, nuts, and dried berries to the dough for additional texture and flavor. I love using toasted pepitas (pumpkin seeds). Sunflower seeds work well, too.

You'll need:

1/2 cup dry multigrain cereal mix (Bob's Red Mill works great)

1 and 3/4 cups boiling water

1 tablespoon instant or active dry yeast (or 1 standard flat square packet)

3 tablespoons packed dark brown sugar

3 tablespoons butter, softened to room temperature

1 and 1/2 teaspoons salt

3 and 1/3 cups <u>bread</u> flour plus more as needed and for hands/work surface

Other additions, if you like: 1/2 cup sunflower seeds, chopped nuts, pepitas, or dried cranberries

One egg white, for brushing over the top of the loaf, if you want to add seeds or nuts to it.

1. Place the cereal mix in a large bowl (you can also use a sturdy glass bowl or the bowl of your stand mixer). Pour boiling water on top. Let the mixture cool until you can put your finger in it easily.

2. Mix the yeast, sugar, and all of the warm water-cereal mixture in the bowl of your stand mixer fitted with a dough hook or paddle attachment. Cover and allow it to sit for 5-10 minutes or until it's foamy and bubbly.

3. Now add the butter, salt, and one cup of the flour. Beat on low speed for 30 seconds, then scrape down the sides of the bowl with a silicone spatula and add another cup of flour. Beat on medium speed until blended (there may still be bits of butter). Add all of the remaining flour along with the seeds and/or nuts (if using), then beat on medium speed until the dough comes together and pulls away from the sides of the bowl--about 2 minutes. If it seems too sticky,

add more flour, one tablespoon at a time until it begins to pull away from the sides of the bowl.

<u>Note:</u> If you don't have a stand mixer, you can mix this dough with a wooden spoon or silicone spatula. It's a lot of work, but you can do it!

4. <u>Knead the dough</u>: Keep the dough in the mixer and beat for an additional 3-5 minutes or knead by hand on a lightly floured surface for 3-5 minutes. After kneading, the dough should still feel a little soft. Poke it with your finger—if it slowly bounces back, your dough is ready to rise.

5. <u>First rise</u>: Lightly grease a large bowl with olive oil or nonstick spray. Place the dough in the bowl, turning it to coat all sides in the oil. Cover the bowl with plastic wrap or a clean kitchen towel. Allow the dough to rise in a warm place for 1-2 hours or until it's doubled in size.

6. Grease a 9×5-inch loaf pan.

7. <u>Shape the bread</u>: When the dough is ready, punch it

down to release the air. Lightly flour a work surface, your hands, and a rolling pin. Roll the dough into a large rectangle, roughly 8 by 15 inches. It will be a little rounded on the edges. Roll it up into an 8-inch log and place in the loaf pan.

8. <u>Second rise:</u> Cover the top of the shaped loaf with plastic wrap or a clean kitchen towel. Allow it to rise until it's about 1-2 inches above the top of the loaf pan--about 1 hour.

9. Adjust the oven rack to the center of the oven and preheat oven to 350°F (177°C).

10. If you want to adorn the top of your loaf, brush the top with egg white, then sprinkle a light coat of seeds or nuts over it.

11. Bake the bread for 35-40 minutes. If the top is browning too quickly during bake time, lay aluminum foil over the top. To test for doneness, give the loaf a light tap. If it sounds hollow, it's done.

12. Remove from the oven and let the bread cool for an hour before slicing and serving. The aroma will make you want to dig in earlier, but don't! It will get gummy if it's not fully cooled.

Cover the leftover bread tightly and store at room temperature for 2-3 days or in the refrigerator for up to 10 days.

Bucatini Alla Amatriciana

Time needed: 45 minutes to an hour

This pasta dish is easy, really flavorful, and a favorite of Nate, Gracie's boyfriend. You don't have to use bucatini, a thick noodle with a tube running through it. Regular spaghetti works just fine.

Bucatini Alla Amatriciana

You'll need:
8 ounces of unsliced guanciale (cured beef cheek) or
pancetta
1-1/2 tablespoons olive oil
1 medium red onion, peeled and coarsely chopped
24-ounce can of Italian tomatoes
½ teaspoon hot red-pepper flakes
Salt and freshly ground black pepper
16 ounces of dried bucatini (or spaghetti)
½ to 3/4 cup freshly grated Romano or Parmesan cheese

1. If it isn't already, cut the guanciale or pancetta into small chunks less than one-half inch thick. Place in a saucepan with the olive oil and fry over **low heat** for about 15 minutes, until the meat is just crisp. Make sure you watch them so they don't burn. Remove the meat from the pan and set aside.

2. Add the chopped onion to the pan and saute over medium heat for five minutes.

3. Roughly chop the tomatoes, then add them and the tomato liquid to the onion in the pan. Season with red-pepper flakes and salt and pepper to taste and simmer 20 minutes, stirring occasionally.

4. Bring a large pot of cold water to a boil and add salt to taste. Add the pasta and cook until *al dente*, about 9 to 11 minutes. Drain very well.

5. Transfer the cooked sauce to a big, heavy skillet over medium-high heat. Add the pasta and the cooked guanciale or pancetta and cook, stirring, for about a minute. Remove the skillet from the heat. Add the cheese and mix very well. Transfer the pasta to a warm bowl or platter, serve—and eat!
Makes 4 to 6 servings

Are you in a book club?

Interested in reading any of *The Laughing Loaf Bakery Mysteries* or *Silicon Valley Murder* series with your book club? I'd love to appear at your book club online - or possibly in person, if you're in the San Francisco Bay Area. Contact me at thelaughingloaf@gmail.com